His Second Chance

FIANCÉE

JULIETTE HYLAND

Copyright © 2024 by JH Publishing

All rights reserved.

No part of this book may be reproduced in any form or by any electronic or mechanical means, including information storage and retrieval systems, without written permission from the author, except for the use of brief quotations in a book review. No part of this book is authorized for use training artificial intelligence (AI).

This is a work of fiction. References to real people, events, establishments, organizations, or locales are intended only to provide authenticity, and are used fictitiously. All other characters, and all incidents and dialogue, are drawn from the author's imagination and are not to be construed as real.

For those who never give up on a dream.

Chapter One

THE STORE CLOCK'S chime set Natasha Saddler's heart to racing. Splatters of dirt and unidentified grime stained her cleaning overalls long ago. Setting aside the broom, she forced herself to ignore the final dust bunnies in the corner. Her bun passed the cute-but-messy stage hours ago, and she'd chipped two fingernails.

There goes the manicure splurge. Serves me right.

Most of Walkins, Wyoming's residents were accustomed to her untidy appearance when she operated Saddler's Farm Supply, but tonight needed to be different. *She* needed to be different. If her business expansion was going to succeed, the community needed to see her as Natasha Saddler, entrepreneur. The apple-red dress and fancy belt she bought for her open house whispered from their perch in the stock-room. This was going to work.

It has to.

Nope. Natasha would not let more worries in. Hell, there was a whole nest of them in her brain already, despite the mental eviction notices she'd given.

The bell rang, and she halted to glare at her watch. It was too early for guests. Reluctantly changing course, Natasha kept her mutterings under her breath about some people's inability to read signs. She clenched her fists and forced a smile as she called out, "Sorry, we're closed."

"Door was open." The rich voice. The deep tones. A subtle, Midwest accent.

Natasha's brain screamed at her heart as it skipped a beat. *Finnegan?*

It wasn't him. Was never him. Her ex-fiancé hadn't returned to Walkins in almost a decade. And the last place she needed him was here—*tonight.*

There was plenty left unsaid between them. But that was the way the world worked. If he came looking for a long-awaited talk, she certainly wasn't doing it now. He'd walked away once he could turn on his heel and take himself right out the door. *And out of my life.*

She was walking towards the front just to reinforce that they were closed. Even if it was him.

Finnegan leaned against the counter with his arms crossed. His dark, brown eyes skirted over her, and his mouth twitched. Was he laughing at her or smiling?

Doesn't matter, Nat. Natasha tucked her chin, forcing her tongue to unstick from the roof of her mouth. He needed to leave.

"We are hosting a friends and family night event in about thirty minutes. I've closed the registers." Natasha yearned to turn on her heel and walk off. Like he'd done to her. However, with his uncle's passing, Finnegan owned Nightfall Ranch. She doubted he planned to keep it, but on the tiny chance he might, she couldn't afford to turn away business. "I'd be happy to get you anything you need when we reopen Monday."

Finnegan's fingers tightened on his biceps, but he didn't move. "I think I qualify as friends and family, Natasha."

Her cheeks heated under his traveling gaze. How many times had she replayed their reunion in her head? More than she wanted to admit. Never once had she imagined greeting him in oversized, dusty overalls. Why should life be fair?

"I fail to see how, Finnegan." Her heart fluttered as his name slipped from her lips. He shouldn't still affect her. He left. He did not deserve to come home and make her wish for things. Natasha should order him out of her store. She'd spent too many years loving him, waiting for him, cursing him. However, her tongue refused to say the words her brain supplied.

Not bothering with discretion, Natasha lifted her wrist and huffed at the ever-moving clock hands. Fine, let him stand there all night. She needed out of these grimy clothes before her guests arrived. Catching up with Finnegan was not on her calendar.

Not tonight. Not ever.

Instead of taking the hint, the man fell into step with her. She glared at him as she halted. The last thing she needed was him following her into the back.

Her fingers tingled as heat traveled across her neck. Finnegan was here. Back in Walkins. And Nat hated the parts of her soul that cried for him to leave, almost as much as she hated the tiny bubble of hope that he might want to stay.

Time transformed his boyish good looks into chiseled handsomeness holding the faint echo of power. His body was still slim, but the lines around his dark eyes were harder than she remembered. Finnegan's curly hair was unkempt, and his jeans hung loosely on his frame. Was he eating enough? Probably not. No doubt, running a successful tech startup was draining.

Glancing at Finnegan, her memory flooded with times his large hands had found hers. Nope. No. Those were exactly the sort of memories she was not diving into.

That man was gone. This one was a stranger.

His lips trembled, and his eyes were bloodshot. Grief did weird things to people. Despite his long absence, he came home to an empty ranch. His uncle, the man who raised him, was a memory. And nothing more. Forever.

She missed Warren, too, and she had more than enough time to say goodbye. He was kind. A stalwart member of the community. Everyone in Walkins missed him. And they weren't related to him.

Her heart defrosted a tad as she studied Finnegan's haggard features. He carried himself the same way his uncle had. Despite their differences, Natasha wished she could welcome Finnegan home with some form of comfort. A hug or something, but the bridge dividing them was too long for her to cross.

Cocking his head to the side, Finnegan shrugged. "Sorry for interrupting, I'm only going to be in town for a little while. I've kept odd hours the last few years, and I lost track of time. When I saw the lights still on? I just stopped in. Old habit, I guess. Sorry. It's good to see you, Nat."

Some of her anger receded as her nickname tripped off his tongue. Offering him a weak smile, she almost reached for him before catching herself. "There is a lot of work needed at Nightfall Ranch, Finnegan."

"I prefer to go by Finn now. It's easier to remember, sounds more professional."

"My apologies, *Finn.*" The brief spell broke as the distance he placed between them registered. Raising an eyebrow, Natasha refrained from rolling her eyes. Barely. She knew it was petty, but she couldn't help but add, "If I don't know your preferred name, then I doubt we can really call ourselves friends."

Soft hands clasped her wrist. Finn's thumb hovered over her tender skin as his eyes met hers. "I figure we used to make out in the employee break room. Surely, that qualifies me for Saddler's gathering."

How dare he be so flippant about their past. Pulling away

from his touch, she crossed her arms. Finn's eyes refused to meet hers as he studied his shoes.

Good, he should be ashamed!

"I need to get ready. You're not the only one with a business to run." She would not interrupt her life for Finnegan Matus. Not again. "Stick around, *if* you know how."

Why was she taunting him? Her stomach clenched, but she didn't feel like apologizing either. There was no point in waiting for a reply. Yes, it was a cowardly retreat, but she didn't look back.

How did a woman look so sexy in oversized overalls? In his absence, Natasha completed her transition from a cute, young adult to a strikingly beautiful woman. Her curly, red hair bundled on her head, and her nose speckled with those freckles from hours spent outside. Just like he remembered. Nat's gray eyes showed no signs of the love and affection a part of him foolishly hoped to see.

That was the past. Finn knew that, but he'd never been able to push Natasha Saddler from his mind. Seeing her unraveled him. He crossed his arms to keep from reaching out to her or seeking comfort. Despite the years of silence, if he'd reached for her, she'd hold him while he mourned the man who'd raised him. She might hesitate, but Nat was too friendly, too loving, too perfect.

Too perfect for me.

How long had it been since someone had held Finnegan Matus? Since he allowed anyone to get close? With his company's success came leeches, and he feared anyone offering kindness, or friendship, expected him to reward the act.

In San Francisco, he called the shots, but here in Walkins, everyone saw him as the orphaned son of the town's wild children. The man who turned his back on the town that molded him, the uncle who parented him, and the woman who loved him.

His response to her could have been less defensive. There was no need to be a jerk. It didn't matter if Nat called him Finnegan, Finn, or any other name. Blowing out a breath, he tried to remind his heart this was a quick trip, not a romantic comedy movie. Nat had her life here. If he didn't go back to San Francisco in the next few days, his board might use his absence to take over one. With each lucrative buyout offer landing in their inbox, his control of his company slipped further. Finn was not about to let them steal his victory.

Finn pushed off every takeover attempt. So far. He sacrificed everything to found Reach. If he gave up, what would he have left? A pile of money, an empty house, and a phone full of business contacts that would only answer if he had another business idea, they could make millions off.

There was nothing in Wyoming for him. Not anymore. After he missed Warren's funeral, he booked another flight and canceled it. Then, he repeated the exercise three times until this morning. If he wasn't honor-bound to walk through Nightfall Ranch before he sold it, he wouldn't have come back.

Part of him needed to say goodbye. To close this part of life forever.

"Well, well, Finnegan Matus has finally come home." Herb Saddler returned the smile, but he didn't hide the effort it cost him. Refusing to correct anyone else, Finn smiled at Nat's father as he emerged from the back of the store. "We were all saddened by your uncle's passing. His funeral *was* well attended."

The rebuke stung. Finn kept his eyes focused on one of the store's shelves. His chest burned as the weight of the words dropped their barbs deep in his soul. Uncle Warren never hesitated when the call came to take in a sad, young child. He'd been Finn's biggest champion, and Finn hadn't made it home for the funeral. *Or any other time.*

Finn hadn't truly believed Warren was gone until arriving at Nightfall. Crossing the ranch's silent threshold, Finn hadn't bothered to contain the pain ripping through him. He'd sat on the front stoop for almost an hour, hating himself.

Why did I wait so long to come home?

He chased the tech dreams that refused to materialize here. In California, they blossomed. However, he didn't intend to stay away so long. If Warren had asked Finn to come home, he would've gotten on the next flight.

He was angry with his uncle, too. The man kept so much to himself. Too kind, and proud, to beg his wayward nephew to spend a few weeks with him. Now it was too late.

A lifetime of what-ifs haunted Finn.

"Thank you, sir. I'm sure it was a lovely service" he choked out the words, unable to hold the big man's gaze.

He'd meant to come. Finn really had. A meeting with his board went on late into the night, and he'd overslept. If he hadn't booked a flight that landed a few hours before the service?

"I think it is past time you called me Herb." Natasha's father tapped Finn on the back, studiously pretending to ignore the mist forming in his eyes. Herb's steps were slow, and his back was bent.

The last year had been a blur while he prepared for his company's rollout of an operating system that rivaled the best in the business for a third of the cost. In the weeks following the system's success, three companies expressed an interest in acquiring Reach. The pinnacle of Finn's success meant the vultures were circling with obscene sums of money the other board members had little interest in ignoring.

"What brings you into the store?"

"I need some things for Uncle Warren's ranch. There's not much there."

Why did I say that? The ranch was bare, but it was fine for the few days he'd be in town. Three days. Tops. He hadn't even meant to come to Saddler's. It had just happened. Mostly, his soul needed to see Nat.

"Everything Nightfall needs is on a list in the bottom, right-hand drawer. Main register," Natasha's voice lilted through the room as she reemerged from the back. Her eyes darted to Finn's, and her teeth pulled at her bottom lip as she hesitated before adding, "I didn't know if you would return."

Finn's brain was incapable of forming thoughts. Every cell focused on the beauty before him. If he thought the overalls were attractive?

Nat's knee-length candy-apple red dress swirled as she walked, showcasing a pair of well-worn cowboy boots. A thick, white leather belt highlighted her trim waist, and her hair hung in a loose ponytail off to the side. She'd painted her lips to match the dress.

The look was softer than he saw on the west coast. And sexy as hell. Finn drank in the image before him. Nat's soft cough alerted him to the seconds of no conversation while he not-so-subtly checked her out.

"How do you know what Nightfall needs?" His voice was hoarse, and he pulled the loose collar of his shirt, trying to ignore the lightning ripping through his chest. No one expected him to come home. *Not even Warren.*

Gracefully moving to adjust some cut daisies on a table with a mountain of cookies, she took a minute before looking over her shoulder. "I took care of Warren as his health failed. After he passed, I put together a list of things Nightfall needed, in case you returned. As the executor of his will, it seemed prudent."

She wasn't the executor.

Couldn't be. Finn's mind refused to accept her simple admission. "According to my lawyer, the executor is my uncle's wife. Not that Warren really ever spoke of her." Not that he knew much about the will.

His lawyer had set up multiple appointments to discuss it. But Finn hadn't wanted to discuss it. He knew the basics. He got Nightfall. The widow Matus was the executor but got nothing else. Finding out everything meant his uncle was really gone.

And Finn hadn't wanted to face that. So he'd focused on the widow. Fury at the idea that she'd married a terminal bachelor fueling him. There was no reason for it except to get the ranch. "Must have hoped my uncle would leave her the farm and money. Must have come as a nasty surprise to find that he left everything to his wayward nephew."

"Finn." There was a look in her eye. Sympathy? Pity? Worry. "Finnegan, I," her hand reached for him but when her words died the action did to. She wrapped her hands around her waist. "It wasn't a surprise."

His ears buzzed as his brain tried to make sense of what she was saying. Uncle Warren had been a confirmed bachelor. The man never showed interest in a partner. After living in San Francisco, Finn wondered if the man may have been asexual.

It wouldn't have mattered. However, finding out Warren had married. *And said nothing?*

Finn had always hoped his uncle might find love. He would have gladly accepted a new person into their family, but Warren never acted like a man in love. He never spoke of a bride or anyone else. *Not that I asked.*

Finn pressed on, trying to force some of the bitterness from his voice. "I didn't even get invited to their wedding."

Warren treated his marriage casually. He informed Finn of his marital status following a suggestion that Warren should hire help, if the ranch was tiring him out. Finn maintained a wall of silence for three months.

Three months gone, when he'd only had twelve left.

Fighting to sound cheery, he continued, "That is tomorrow's problem, though. No doubt in a town this small, one young, widow shouldn't be too hard to find."

"Finnegan," Herb's voice caught as he stared at his daughter.

This wasn't happening. It wasn't. There was no way. None. "Nat?" Her name fell like lead, but she kept her eyes rooted firmly on the concrete floor.

She let out a soft sigh. "Finn."

Heat stole across his skin as he tried to will her to look at him. Anger warred with jealousy. No. It wasn't possible.

"You married Warren." The words were too loud. No. His chest was caving in. The room was spinning. This wasn't happening. It wasn't. There was no reason. "Why? Hoping to get Nightfall's land for your family?"

"Wait just a minute." Herb started towards Finn, but Natasha raised her hand to stop him. For a moment, Finn thought tears glistened behind her long lashes, but her eyes were clear as she straightened her back and met his gaze.

"Tonight is not the night for this discussion. I have most of the town coming to hear about Saddler's business expansion."

Manic laughter erupted from Finn's chest. "The friends and family night. Guess I qualify as family now."

A ringing noise behind him interrupted the tirade, and suddenly, tiny arms enveloped him in a hug. Turning, he tried to place the slim, older woman as she patted his cheek.

"Finnegan, you came home," the trim, elderly woman's eyes teared as he tried to remember her name.

Natasha came to his rescue. "Mrs. Dyer, it is so good to see you up and about." She took the older woman by the hand.

"Just so you know, Finnegan prefers to go by Finn now. He finds it more professional."

As she steered their first-grade teacher toward a plate of cookies, she shot him a warning glance. He could control himself for an evening, but tomorrow, Nat was going to answer his questions.

Natasha!

Warren's coarse scream echoed through her brain. Launching out of bed, Natasha reached for the light.

What time was it? How long since Warren's last dose? Why weren't his monitors beeping? Was the power out? Why hadn't the generator kicked on?

Stumbling, Nat ignored the burn chasing across her big toe as she flipped the light switch. Rubbing her eyes, she stared at the tangle of sheets on her bed.

Her bed. In her apartment. Not at the ranch. It was a dream. Again. "Damn it."

There were no monitors, no medicine to dispense, no responsibilities. Sliding down the wall, Natasha cradled her head in her arms. *And no Warren.*

For nearly three years, alarms dominated her nights. During the day, insurance paid for a visiting nurse. However, insurance refused to clear around the clock care until the week before he passed. The kind nurse's first night had been Warren's last. She'd helped Natasha wait for the authorities and fill out the mountains of paperwork that appeared in the hours after. Nat had been grateful not to be alone, but the young woman hadn't served with in the trenches of Warren's final weeks.

Eight weeks. Eight weeks since that last night. No meds due. No monitors to track. No reason to get out of bed in the middle of the night.

And still her body refused to give her eight hours uninterrupted.

Clenching her jaw, she glared at her bed. Finn's face danced before her eyes, and her lungs burned as her body shook. It wasn't fair that Warren was gone, and Finn was back.

Nothing about these last few weeks was easy. Nat accepted her widowhood the day she and Warren met at the courthouse. It wasn't a love match, but rather a better way for an old friend to guarantee access to records and support only a spouse could claim.

Her shoulders shook. Fury poured through her veins as she stared at her bed. She was angry, sad, and so tired. It was only three, so Natasha might eke out another hour, maybe two. *This is really Warren's fault.*

The thought ripped through her brain. Her eyes stung, but no tears materialized. Why couldn't she cry? Once upon a time she cried so much it embarrassed her. Hell, even watching a dog food commercial was enough to get her misty. Now? Nothing. Grief and guilt warred within her, and yet her body refused to let her weep.

Charcoal, Warren's ancient barn cat who had never stayed a day in the barn, rubbed up against her. His gray tail softly traced against her legs, and his head rubbed insistently at her hand. Lifting him, she sat him on her lap. At least something still needed her. The small cat's soft purrs filled the silent room as she leaned her head against the wall.

Warmth spread against Natasha's cheek. Turning to greet the morning sun, her neck resisted. Her body locked down, and Nat let out a groan. Her muscles were angry, but at least she'd managed a few extra hours of sleep.

It wasn't like this was the first time she slept on the floor. Taking a deep breath, she wiggled her toes. Forcing blood back into her limbs with each tiny movement, she ignored her body's cry to stay put. The longer she was here, the worse it would be.

Pins and needles raced up her legs, and Nat pushed herself off the wall. Her back and legs screamed, but stopping was not an option. A hot shower and a few over the counter painkillers might not fix everything, but it would be a good start. Then coffee!

And finally Finn.

He'd be over today. Probably soon. She needed composure and caffeine.

Glancing at the clock, Finn sighed and lugged himself off the couch. A blanket tangled around his legs, and he landed in a heap at the foot of the sofa, letting out several curse words into the empty ranch. Disentangling himself, he glanced at the pile of sheets and then stumbled towards the kitchen.

"Not the best way to start the day." Maybe he'd function better after a cup, or liter, of coffee.

The stack of papers detailing Warren's desires for his worldly possessions stared at Finn from the dining room table, where he'd left them. Glowering at the bottom of the coffee tin, Finn slammed it onto the counter. Why hadn't he picked up a few things at the grocery store? Had he expected everything to be waiting for him when he got home?

Home.

The word ricocheted around his brain. Walkins wasn't

home. At least, not anymore. Finn lived in San Francisco. That was his home.

Small-town life was Nat's dream. For a while, he tried to pretend it was his, too, or that it could be. His attempts to launch his company here had failed. Repeatedly.

If he secured financing, things might have turned out differently. Finn had met with every potential investor in Walkins and the surrounding area. They had said no. Most in delicate, Midwest polite ways, before the meeting even really got started. More than one local had compared him to his parents.

Fond words flowed about how he looked like the wild children the town had lost so long ago. Words that turned to into direct 'not interested' when he redirected the conversation towards investing in his company. Finn wasn't reckless, and his business could have succeeded here, if anyone had believed in him.

When he'd expressed his frustration at the town's unwillingness to change, Nat had offered him an alternative. She'd outlined her plans to advance Saddler's grow it into a nationwide chain. Then, she tried to convince him that expanding Saddler's wasn't giving up on his dreams but rather adjusting them.

But what else was it?

Nat's eyes had sparkled with dreams he hadn't wanted. He'd packed his bags that night, asked Nat to come with him, and tried to push away the hurt when she told him he was being hasty. She hadn't believed in him. That stung, but Finn forced himself not to look back. That was a lost dream he couldn't afford to examine.

Nat belonged in Walkins. This town needed her as much as she needed it. He'd known it then and saw it again last night. *Why didn't she have a couple of kids and a doting husband?*

She was supposed to be happy, not his uncle's widow.

Warren's widow. The wife he never mentioned. The woman who had worn his ring.

How often had they laughed? Shared meals at the table? Cried together? His knuckles popped before he released his grip on the sink. No good could come from those thoughts.

Rolling his neck, Finn picked up the papers he'd attempted to wade through after Natasha's event. Following Warren's marriage, Finn assumed the holdings would transfer to Warren's wife. It annoyed his nephew that someone might marry the old bachelor for their own gain, but Warren had known Finn's destiny wasn't in Walkins. *So why leave the ranch to me? Natasha.*

His ears burned as he rifled through stacks of legal papers he'd never actually read. Why had his she done this?

She stopped being *his* years ago. Swallowing the lump catching in his throat, Finn focused on the task at hand. The sooner he sold the ranch, the faster he could go back to his company.

The legal language in his uncle's will was straightforward. If he'd listened to his lawyer or read the documents before showing up at Sadler's he could have at least avoided Nat witnessing his shock.

Following the words on the page, Finn pushed back at the bitterness coating his chest. Nat was to receive a small stipend for acting as the estate's executor. The will never referred to Natasha as Warren's wife, though. It read as though she was a business associate. Sighing, he put the will aside and lifted the other paper he'd found pinned to the corkboard in the kitchen.

Instructions for the disposal of Nightfall Ranch, in the likely event my heir, Finnegan Reed Matus, does not have the time, or inclination, to return to Walkins. The livestock has been sold, and my executor has access to the deeds. I request all assets be sold to pay any debts owed. Any leftover funds should be transferred to the following charities on my behalf.

Finn's headache had faded, but the words still burned. Uncle Warren never expected him to return to claim any of his inheritance. Finn didn't need money, a fact Warren knew, but surely Warren had believed his nephew would return to say goodbye. Except he hadn't made it to the funeral. Reach came first. His company *always* came first.

Nat's face floated in his gaze. It wasn't just Reach that kept him away. Fear of seeing her with someone else had prevented him from returning to Walkins, too. Finn asked about her during each of his calls home. His uncle had never been very forthcoming, giving him just the basics. "Nat's well. You should call her."

He'd wanted to scream for more details, even knowing that it would break him when she finally pledged herself to another. Of course, Warren hadn't told him about their union. How would Finn have responded?

Warren hadn't been himself for at least five years. Looking around the comfortable farm kitchen, Finn felt cowardly for not coming when Warren seemed to drift away during phone conversations. In California, he wore busy as a badge of honor. Finn never took a vacation. Never left for a long weekend, never went some place for fun, or made time to see the few people who mattered. *How can I? They're all here.*

Stewing over the past wouldn't fix anything. His plans hadn't changed. He needed to go back to California. "Reach needs me."

Bile coated his tongue. His oft-repeated phrase sounded hollow in the lonely kitchen. Warren had needed Finn. Natasha had needed him once, too.

Finn stood. It was time he had a long discussion with his uncle's widow.

Natasha dressed and pulled her wet hair into a ponytail. Cringing at her unkempt appearance in the mirror, she raced toward the stairs. She'd heard the banging on her door as soon as she turned off the shower. It went onward still.

Only Finn would hammer on her door for so long. She expected him, but not for another hour or so. At least she had taken a shower before facing him.

"Open the door, Natasha." Finn's growl reached her as she grabbed the door handle. "Nat!"

Looking at her watch, Natasha frowned. She couldn't risk letting Finn's drama draw attention from Mrs. Yeager. Her landlady, and the duplex's other resident, usually left for church early, but if she was home, she might call the police. Nat didn't feel like dealing with additional gossip.

Forcing a smile, she took a deep breath and opened the door. "Good morning, Finn. I apologize for the delay, but I prefer not to answer the door dressed in a towel."

Exhaustion coated Finn's gaze. When had he last shaved? The subtle beard growth would be attractive, if his other features looked less haunted. He looked at her before stomping toward her kitchen.

"Some people might consider it rude to barge into another's home," Natasha huffed back at him and took her time closing the door. He was mourning Warren, but did Finn have to take his anger out on her? *There's no one else for him here.*

"Would a cup of coffee unruffle your feathers?"

When he growled and refused to answer, she moved towards the cabinet without waiting for his response.

"You don't appear to be a grieving widow." The words she heard others whisper slapped her as they fell from his lips.

How was she supposed to act? Her Finnegan would never have been so cruel. Except this wasn't her Finnegan. Finn was a stranger.

Charcoal sauntered up and head bonked against her hand

before he swiped at the counter. He wanted a treat, but she took a moment to pet him, calming her nerves for the moment she dreaded since the day Warren got his diagnosis.

She gave herself a few seconds, and then Nat straightened her back. This was her home, and she was not going to take his vitriol. "I will have a civil discussion with you regarding my marriage to Warren. However, if your purpose this morning is to use me as your emotional punching bag, leave. Or you could take the coffee, like a civilized adult, so we can talk about why you're here."

Finn opened his mouth and shut it. His head bowed, and he closed his eyes for a few seconds. When he opened them, he took the mug from her outstretched hand. Sliding into the seat across from him, Natasha sipped her coffee, letting the silence envelop them. She was comfortable with silence after years in Warren's house, but this wasn't his sickroom.

Nat knew the protocol for helping Warren, routines to follow, medicines to administer, and so much more. What she hadn't prepared for was Finn's arrival, his shock, and how part of her wished he would hold her and tell her things would be alright.

The clock ticked as Finn drank his coffee and traced lines cut into her beat-up table. "I'm sorry, Natasha. I am so terribly sorry, for so many things."

His voice was flat, and Natasha held her tongue, unsure what words to offer. When Finn met her gaze, tears highlighted the hickory tone of his eyes. He brushed them away before leaning his head back. Her stomach churned as she stared at the wet splotches on his cheeks. Why could the prodigal son cry for Warren when she could not?

Warren asked her to help Finn when he returned. But Warren wasn't the one dealing with Finn's anger and grief. She'd promised Warren, but she hadn't expected Finn to come home. *If I had?*

Natasha threw the thought away without completing it.

She reached across the table and grabbed Finn's hand. He allowed her to squeeze it once before he pulled away. She'd crossed the bridge, and he'd pulled back. He was the one who pulled away without a word. The one who abandoned her. Yet he got to be angry.

Why can't I hate him? Or at least be indifferent.

"I need to know why you married Warren." Without waiting for her to answer, Finn pushed his chair back and began pacing the tiny kitchen. Given the length of his legs, four steps were all he could manage before turning around. "Uncle Warren didn't even invite me."

"Would you have come?"

"I…" His lips twisted, and he held up his hands after staring at her, "I… "

Natasha elected to save him from deciding whether to lie or admit that nothing except Warren's death was ever going to drag him back to Walkins.

"We didn't invite anyone, for what it's worth. A courthouse wedding with the judge and the clerk present as a witness." She motioned for him to take his seat before continuing, "I suggested Warren inform you immediately. He didn't always listen to me."

Finn let out a soft chuckle. "Some things never change. He was stubborn as a mule."

Natasha laughed with him. The mood in the room lifted, and she knew Warren would have appreciated the giggles.

"Did you love him?" Finn's question hovered in the stillness.

Natasha bit her lip, releasing it when the tang of blood filled her mouth. How often in the weeks after her wedding had friends asked her that question? In the initial days, she'd skirted the subject, but facing the man who haunted her dreams? She found her standard reply impossible to utter.

"In a way." Shadowed eyes bore into hers as she twisted the spoon in her coffee cup. How did one explain the connection she and Warren had? The words were inadequate. Their love wasn't romantic, but they united during his cancer fight. She didn't love him, but she cared about him.

Finn rolled the coffee cup through his hands as he stared at her. "And that means?"

"Warren was very special to me, but I didn't love him in the way you're asking, and he didn't love me that way either."

"Then why marry? Why, Nat?"

The reality of what Natasha had to tell him hit her. Since the day she'd signed her marriage license, she had dreaded no other moment, not even Warren's death, as much as this one. "His terminal diagnosis came three years ago."

Finn's eyes widened. "No. That can't be right."

"He should've told you, but," Natasha let out an angry sigh. Why had Warren left this unfinished? It wasn't her mess to clean up. "He didn't want you to worry or feel obligated to come home. He was alone, and the difficulties of managing his own care were impossible."

Finn downed the rest of his coffee and pushed his mug aside. "That still doesn't explain why you married him."

"He needed help, but as his friend, I only had so much leverage. It was easier to navigate the intricacies of the medical world as his wife. I could also cover Warren under my health insurance. His policy covered a small portion of the costs, and he hated the idea of selling Nightfall. Our marriage allowed us to transfer him to the company policy, despite the preexisting diagnosis. Better access to care got him well enough to apply for research studies."

"You married my uncle to commit insurance fraud?"

Her chest burned as she tried to remind herself to breathe. That wasn't technically true, but Finn was too sad and furious to listen, even if she could utter the right words. Warren had been one of the few people who understood the hole left by Finn's departure. With his family gone, Natasha welcomed the aging bachelor into hers, and his diagnosis gutted the entire Saddler clan. He'd needed her like Finn never had, but there was no way she'd let those words loose.

"I'm worth millions, Nat. I would have helped. Warren would never have had to sell Nightfall. He didn't *need* to marry you." Finn shook his head as he pulled at his collar. Tears coated his eyes as he stared at her. "Warren married rather than seek my help. Guess he assumed I was too absorbed in my own life to help."

"That's not true."

Finn ignored her interruption as he stalked towards the door. "You could have asked me, too. Instead, you married a sick man knowing you were going to bury him. We were close." His voice cracked as he met her gaze. "And you never called."

That accusation was true. Natasha should have called, but hearing Finn's voice, telling him that she was married? She'd never gained the courage to pick up the phone. Her fingers trembled as she set her coffee down. Grabbing his arm, Natasha tried to make him understand. "We all should have done things differently, Finnegan, but Warren needed someone to care for him in his final days. He didn't want to be alone when he died. You'd have felt honor bound to come home."

"Yes," Finn's exclamation echoed around the small room.

"And you would have hated every minute." Natasha's stomach clenched as she said the words. She didn't wait for him to offer a fake denial or agreement. "Warren knew Reach was important to you, as important as Nightfall was to him. If you came home, he wanted it to be to see him, not to be his caregiver. He should have given you the option to choose, but for what it is worth, he never regretted his choice."

She watched him flinch but refused to release her hold on him. "When we first received his diagnosis, the doctors gave him less than six months."

His jaw clenched as he shook off her hold. "No. I talked to Warren almost every weekend. He never said anything!"

If Warren was here, she might flay him. "I know. It was the fight Warren and I had most often. He said your life was too important to worry about a sick, old man."

"Oh, but your life wasn't too busy because nothing ever happens in this town. You had nothing but free time."

She tried to let the words flow, but her soul was heavy. Warren was gone, and Finn couldn't bring him back. Lashing out at others was part of the grief cycle, but it didn't stop the hurt cutting across her skin.

"Finnegan."

He flinched as she reached for him again, and her heart tore open. Wrapping her arms around herself, Natasha stepped back. She couldn't force him to stay. She learned that long ago. "With experimental treatments, he fought for three more years."

Instead of hearing her further, he slammed the door shut on his way out.

Finn cringed as the door shuddered behind him. Guilt rolled through his stomach. He should have put more than coffee in his belly. Nat helped Warren, cared for him in his final day, because she was Nat. His perfect Nat. Who he'd yelled at and stormed out of her home.

He should turn around and apologize, but his feet refused to change direction. If he walked back in, then he'd beg her to hold him while he figured out the cascade of emotions roiling through him. When she said no, as she should, it would crush him.

And if she said yes?

Finn's heart couldn't afford that thought. He was not staying in Walkins. Nat was his past, and she was the best part of it. If he was going to survive this, he had to look forward.

The sun burned Finn's face as he raced for his rental car. He needed to relocate away from the town and from her. The feelings he buried years before.

He blew past buildings. It took several minutes to determine a path. There were only so many places to go in Walkins. Finn steered the car towards the outskirts of town. The church spire stood tall in the morning light, and several cars filled the small parking lot.

The cemetery's gate was ajar as he pushed past it. How often had he and his friends played there or done research on the town's founders buried in the front? He held his breath as he made his way towards the fresh plots.

Warren's grave was in the last row. A fresh bouquet of sunflowers lay on the newly-set headstone, along with several wilted flowers and a dried wreath. The simple stone bore his uncle's name and the dates of his birth and death. No ornamentation. It was what Warren would have wanted.

"Of all the women, why Nat? If you needed a partner, did you have to choose her?" The selfish words struck him. Kicking the dirt, Finn waited, uncertain of what to do.

The wind picked up but provided no answers. "I'm sorry. I should have come home and visited regularly. I am so angry with myself, but God help me, I'm furious with you."

The words ached into the emptiness.

"That's natural." The husky voice spooked Finn, and he whirled.

"Heard you were at Saddler's last night."

Finn smiled at Mark Brogan and offered a hand to his old friend. "Mark, good to see you."

Mark shook it, but his eyes held little warmth as they bore through him. "Finn."

Waving a hand in the general direction of the headstones, Finn stared at the horizon. "What brings you in here?"

"Heard someone cursing at a gravestone and figured it had to be you. Warren should have told you lots of things. I'd be mad, too."

Finn didn't know what else to say. The wind kicked up around them, and Finn dug his shoe into the dirt. Maybe he should have brought something. Flowers, a card, or anything that might alleviate his guilt. Crossing his arms, Mark stared at Finn. "If you're done arguing with your uncle's ghost, perhaps you might like to join me at the diner for some breakfast. You look like hell."

Without waiting for a reply, Mark turned and headed out of the cemetery. Finn placed a hand on Warren's stone. He closed his eyes to say a quick goodbye. He tried to promise to return, but the effort seemed false.

The smell of scrambled eggs and bacon wafted from Dahlia's Diner, and Finn's mouth watered. The booth's leather cracked as he pushed the menu aside. Did he want a fried egg or pancakes and bacon? "Still getting your usual?"

Mark rolled his eyes, but he ignored his menu and motioned for a server. "My regular, Marsha. I'd be grateful if you could bring us a kettle of coffee."

"I'll have what he's having." Finn rubbed his hands along his pants. He'd tried every restaurant that served breakfast in San Francisco. No one made fluffy pancakes with crunchy edges like Dahlia's. He never had been able to recreate it. Licking his lips, Finn tapped his fingers on the table. His ears burned as the silence stretched between them.

Lifting his coffee cup, Mark took a long sip before setting it aside. "If you hurt Natasha again, I will break every bone in your body. Even if I have to come to California to do it."

Finn's head snapped back. Twirling his spoon, he stared at

Mark. "Not exactly the welcome home I expected from my best friend."

Mark's eyebrows narrowed, "What on earth makes you think we're friends?"

Confusion rolled through Finn. If Mark disliked Finn so much, why invite him to breakfast? This had been their usual Saturday haunt for years. "Guess I figured growing up together and knowing each other's secrets was enough to bind us through the years."

The patrons at the bar turned as Mark's scoff carried across the tiny diner. He shot them a half-hearted salute. The playful spark disappeared as his eyes locked with Finn's. "That might be enough. If you'd answered your phone, cared about emails, or come back for a visit. Hell, you could have invited me to California. In the last twelve years, I've heard from you how many times, Finn?"

Mark reached out, hadn't he done the same? Sent an email? Made a call? Finn's eyes traced the splotches on the ancient formica. No memories formed. Surely, he had called a few times early on. The years had slipped by, covered in busyness and the fatigue of running his company. Finn hadn't meant to make anyone feel forgotten.

"I asked you to come to breakfast to ensure you don't destroy one of my best friends *again*."

What the hell was Mark talking about? Nat had wanted a life in Walkins, more than a life with him. Time should mute that pain, but it still tore through him. Saddler's was the safer life, and she'd chosen it over him. Their breakup nearly destroyed him. He'd spent his first few months in California, working at least sixteen hours a day, and sometimes closer to twenty, to keep his need to call her away. When he moved his company into its downtown office, Finn had taken a photo and almost emailed it to Nat. Even after she hadn't believed in him. The one person he'd wanted to share his success with.

"I assume you plan to deal with Warren's estate and

return to California." Mark's anger broke through the fog of cluttered memories, and what-ifs, that assaulted Finn's brain for the last dozen years. They heightened into a relentless onslaught since Uncle Warren's death. Finn had no plans for the ranch, and he didn't even understand why Warren had left it to him.

Rubbing his face, Finn shrugged. There was no reason to stay. Nothing for him in Walkins. "My life isn't here. No one even expected me to come home for the funeral."

"And you didn't."

"I know!" Finn's fist connected with the table. He pulled back, appalled at how easily his temper rose these days. He pinched his eyes closed, opened them and started again, "I know all my failings, Mark. I never meant to make anyone feel forgotten, though."

"Not interested in apologies, half-hearted or otherwise." Mark tossed a handful of napkins at him. "I accepted I was one piece of baggage you cut loose. However, Natasha has been through a lot in the last few years, and I refuse to allow you to take advantage of her grief."

"She claims she married Warren to help. Is that true, or is Nat trying to protect my feelings?" His words carried across the room, and several eyes turned towards their booth. Lowering his voice, Finn asked, "Did she love him?"

Why open Pandora's box? Did it matter?

His heartbeat pounded in his ears. If Mark didn't answer, was Finn prepared to beg? It was a selfish question, but he couldn't stop the longing that years, and distance, failed to quench. Mark moved so fast. He wrenched Finn out of the booth before he could fully process the movement.

Mark pushed Finn towards the back entrance. "Keep our breakfast warm, Marsha!"

Finn missed the back step and tumbled into the hard dirt. A rock grazed his cheek, and fire erupted across his soul. None of this was fair. Wiping away the trickle of blood, he glared at Mark. "Warren never told me about their marriage, and I asked about Nat *every time* I called. I may not have probed for in-depth answers, but he willfully kept that secret."

"And he shouldn't have," Mark offered, some of the anger in his voice draining away. "Your uncle was alone and sick. She tried to help him as his friend, but it was hard. She married him to make the process simpler."

"She never asked for my help."

Mark laughed, the bitter sound echoing down the alley. "You didn't answer her phone calls after you left. Why would she think you'd answer years later?"

His chest clenched. That was true. In the early days, he ignored every call knowing if he'd answered he'd have headed right back here. Then he sobbed for a week after the last one ever came. "Nat chose this. She wanted Walkins and Saddler's. I expected her to be happily married."

Mark's face shifted, his lips turning from a hard-set line to a soft frown. "Why would she be married? You left."

Closing his eyes, Finn rocked back on his heels. Was she as lost without him as he'd been without her? Refusing to acknowledge the bloom of hope pooling in his belly, Finn opened his eyes. "If you're going to pummel me, go ahead."

"Don't be ridiculous." Mark snorted, but his lip almost twitched into a smile. "I have no intention of breaking your nose, even if you deserve it."

"Why make me come out to the back alley?" Finn spun around. The smell of eggs and bacon couldn't cover the hint of garbage.

"So, I could yell at you in a semi-private way. Small towns gossip, remember?" Mark kicked the dirt. "Why do you think I should beat the snot out of you?"

Finn bit his lip. He didn't owe Mark an explanation, but the words tumbled forth anyway. "I ran away." It hadn't felt that way, but Finn couldn't deny it. "I couldn't have gotten Reach off the ground here. It's what I wanted."

"But?"

Leave it to Mark to force the issue. "But coming home without Warren feels like such a failure. I never thought of Walkins changing, in my mind, everything was the same."

Pulling at his chin, Finn stared at the two-lane road that led into town. Except it was four lanes and more cars passed on it than ever. "I've argued with Nat twice in the last twenty-four hours. I deserve a solid thrashing. Warren's not here."

He choked, hating the brokenness within him. "I'm lost. Warren was an anchor I didn't know I needed until he was gone."

Mark rubbed his neck. "I can understand that."

"I *am* sorry I let our friendship become one casualty of my decision to leave. It was stupid and immature, I know." Finn offered his hand to Mark.

Mark hesitated before reaching for it. His grip was firm but brief. He pushed his hands into his pockets as soon as he broke the connection. "Come on, Marsha won't keep our food warm forever."

Marsha made no comment as she dropped the two omelets and fruit cups on their table, but she hovered for several seconds. Finn smiled, but Marsha was too busy tapping out a message on her phone to notice. By this afternoon, gossip would report his and Mark's disagreement as a brawl across town.

Cringing, Finn stared in horror at his plate. "What is this? Where are the pancakes?"

"*This* is breakfast. Veggie egg white omelet and fresh fruit. My regular since my father died of clogged arteries five years back." Taking two big bites, Mark smiled. "Time marches on. None of us are the same people we were."

Staring at the coffee dregs in his cup, Finn asked, "After

everything I've done and not done, why didn't you want to kick my butt?"

"You're not worth it. A few years ago, I might have helped you punish yourself. The day I found Natasha inconsolable over your refusal to answer her phone calls, I would have gladly blackened both your eyes and broken your nose. She wouldn't have appreciated it then." Mark hesitated before adding, "Or now."

Hope flared, but he pushed it away. Nat's dreams were more tightly tied to Walkins and Saddler's than they had been when he left. Software companies were in Silicon Valley, or on the east coast, but they weren't in Walkins, Wyoming.

"After a few years, the anger burned through, and I forgot about you," Mark tapped his fork on his plate. "When Warren got ill, and you refused to look past your company and come home, I wrote you off."

"He never told me." Finn choked on the words and kept his eyes focused on the table. "I always thought there would be more time." A tear slipped down his cheek, and he brushed it away. "That's a mistake I can't take back."

Mark nodded. "Your uncle loved you, and he loved Natasha." Mark held up a hand and pressed on, "He loved her as an uncle and appreciated that she put her life on hold to help him. Nat took care of Warren out of friendship and because she once loved you."

Mark's quiet words landed on Finn's soul, and he had to swallow the lump pressing against his throat. "I was so angry when I found out she was his widow. I went over this morning, argued, and stormed out of her house. Slammed the door for effect. Made an ass of myself."

Mark grunted.

"I think we both know the answer to why you're here, and it has nothing to do with Nightfall Ranch or Warren."

"I can't stay." The diner's noise pulsed in Finn's ears as he tried to breathe.

"If that is the case," Mark stood and dropped a few bills on the table. "Apologize to Natasha. You owe her that."

"And then?" Finn asked, knowing the answer as Mark's eyes shifted.

"And *then* cut ties with everything here. Natasha may not get her happily ever after, but she will never have it if she believes it's at all possible that you will come back for her."

Nodding, Finn stood. "I need to go over a few things at Nightfall. Come with me? For old times' sake."

Mark hesitated before shrugging. "Why not? Life always was more exciting when you were in town. Let's just hope the fireworks don't burn us all."

The sun glittered off the empty glass bottles hanging on the front porch. When Warren became confined to bed, Nat ensured a pretty flower stuck out the top of each one. In their emptiness, they looked forlorn and cheap. She should have taken them down.

At least Lauren Aymes's SUV was parked in the driveway. Her best friend always had a way of showing up when anyone needed an extra hand or a simple hug. Lauren opened her car door and waved as Natasha pulled into her usual parking spot.

"I said I didn't need any help," Nat called as she headed up the front steps.

"I'm not great at listening." Lauren jogged up the steps. "Want to talk about it?"

Natasha's nose crinkled. "Finn stopped by my place a while ago. We argued about Warren, and I forgot to mention my plans to clean up a few things. He may frown on our being here, but things still need to be done."

She froze as she entered the kitchen. The documents from

Warren's desk lay in piles on the kitchen table, and a coffee mug sat next to the sink. "Finn's staying here."

Lauren wrapped an arm around Natasha's waist. "It belongs to him, right?"

"Yeah. However, this place is basically bare. He mentioned needing supplies the other night. Still, I assumed he was staying at a motel." The assumption was ridiculous. After all, he had a free ranch house at his disposal. She'd cleaned his room, dusted and put fresh sheets on the bed. But that was to make Warren happy, not because she believed he'd come home.

Lauren crossed her arms. "How did he even get in?"

"Warren refused to change any of the locks. I think he always hoped Finn might choose to just show up one day. Guess he ended up being right in the end."

Spinning her keys, Nat ran her hand over Finn's chair. A part of her had always expected Finn to show up, too. She'd see a dark head of hair in the distance on main street and rush for it. It was never Finn, but part of her heart refused to stop believing.

"He's not staying. Walkins isn't grand enough." After Reach failed the first time, she thought he'd help her with Saddler's, build up their savings and then try to launch the tech company again. Instead, he'd abandoned her. "Walkins isn't designed to launch a major tech company."

Lauren clucked her tongue.

"Something to say?" Cringing at her tone, Nat started. "I'm sorry."

Lauren winked as she interrupted, "I know you love this town, but it's unfair to judge someone for their choices, honey."

Holding up a hand to stall any argument, Lauren continued, "I am partial to Walkins too, but other places are great. People should not be punished for wanting to chase their own dreams."

"You sound like a teacher." Natasha stuck her tongue out.

"Education 101, encourage kids!" The art teacher grinned as she playfully put her hands on her hips. "It is not nice to stick your tongue out at anyone."

Throwing her hands in the air, Natasha spun and moved to Warren's room. She opened the windows. No matter how many times she aired the room out, the antiseptic smell always seeped back in. Swallowing the lump in her throat, Natasha glared at the remnants of Warren's last days. "Thank you for coming."

Shaking her head, Natasha tried to make her feet move. She started this last task several times and never made it longer than a few minutes. This room was still a mess. "I'm not sure we can sell much in here. The sheets and pillows might be okay to donate to the animal shelter, along with some of the other items in the linen closet. The insurance company took the medical equipment it 'loaned' for his care." They'd paid a pretty penny for the equipment each month, but she'd do it again in a heartbeat.

"Are you sure that Finn wants to hold an auction? He might want to keep the ranch."

She couldn't let herself hope. Finn's life was in California.

He left me years ago. She sat on the edge of the bed. "I doubt it. He mentioned nothing about it when he was yelling at me this morning."

"How long did the two of you date?" she asked.

"Warren and I didn't date, Lauren. I was his caretaker, and it was easier to help navigate the medical system as his wife… and for his own safety."

"You're being willfully obtuse," Lauren snapped a towel against Natasha's knee. "The last thing I need is more 'it was easier' lines."

Natasha smiled at her friend's air quotes. "I know you didn't grow up here, but I'm surprised you never heard that gossip."

Lauren wrapped her arms around Natasha's shoulders. "I don't listen to gossip. Everyone has baggage. Finn is yours. You are his."

"There's not much to tell. Finn and I were high school sweethearts. Elementary school sweethearts, truthfully." Natasha laughed at the memories of her following Finn and Mark across the playground and demanding to be included in children's invented games.

"People started joking about us walking down the aisle around the third grade."

"That is horrible."

Lauren's outraged response sent a ripple of laughter through her. "Small town humor. I always forget you grew up… wait. How do I still not know where you grew up?"

"Nice try." Lauren arrived in town to teach four years before and joked that her past wasn't exciting enough to rehash. "We are talking about your elementary school boyfriend. What happened?"

"For the first two decades of my life, Finn was simply there." After he left, Natasha considered purging his image from her life. Her scrapbook had less than ten pictures without him. Destroying that many photos wouldn't bring him back, and Natasha hadn't wanted to lose so much of her past. "It sounds so melodramatic."

Lauren arched an eyebrow and grinned but kept her lips sealed.

"He asked me to a dance when we were thirteen. We graduated high school together and then went to the University of Wyoming. Finn studied computers, and I muddled my way through my agriculture science degree. We scraped by in cheap dorms and, later, cheaper apartments. Dad still thinks I lived with a roommate instead of Finn."

Natasha laughed at the happy memories. Until Reach's second failure in Wyoming, she believed they could conquer anything. The folly of youth. "We were young, frivolous, and not concerned with looking too far into the future."

They had been so young, once. So sure the future was theirs to conquer together. Swallowing, she rubbed her bare ring finger. "He proposed to me on my twentieth birthday and left the week after I turned twenty-three."

"You were engaged for three years?" Lauren's eyes were wide.

Natasha shrugged. "His dreams were bigger than this town, and he knew I wanted a life here. He was upset after Reach failed to get much support in town. I suggested he help me grow Saddler's. He thought California provided him better opportunities."

"Which it did."

Nat's stomach rolled as Finn's angry face floated in her mind. His accusation that she didn't believe in him haunted her dreams. She hadn't meant that he needed to set his dreams aside. Just put them on pause for a few years. Let them get healthy savings to show the investors. Let them see they had resources to fall back on while it was getting off the ground.

That was the argument the bank used against them. Where was the collateral? How were you supposed to have collateral, if you weren't already from wealth? Sure, Saddler's was healthy, and Nightfall ranch was worth more than a million due to the land value alone. However, agriculture came with debt. A bitter truth any farmer could tell.

Her heart ached, but there'd been so many good memories, too. "Let's see if we can salvage any of this."

Grabbing a pair of sheets from the floor, Natasha tossed them into the pile Lauren had started. "Want to go through the closet?"

Ignoring Nat's question, Lauren offered one of her own. "Did you plan much of the wedding?"

The old wound wept as she remembered hovering over invitations, dress shopping, and begging Finn to choose a date. "Not really. I paid for my dress."

"You had a dress?"

Natasha jumped at Finn's unexpected question. "Finn."

He stared at her as he strode through the door. "I refused to set a date. Why did you have a dress?"

"Not the best way to ask," Mark's voice was cold, but steady, as he leaned against the doorjamb.

Nat clenched her fists. Why the hell was Finn popping in at all the wrong times? Why care if she had purchased a dress? None of it had mattered for years. This was not a conversation she wanted to have, particularly with an audience. "What woman doesn't want to pick out her wedding dress after her fiancé proposes? I thought, at the time, that I would get to use it."

Finn opened his mouth, but no words followed the motion. Crimson coated his cheeks, and he rolled from side-to-side on his heels. "Nat."

She cringed as her nickname slipped into the quiet room. Wrapping her arms around herself, she tried to will warmth into her body. She finally met Finn's gaze.

"Natasha," Finn rocked back on his heels and stuffed his hands them into his pockets. "I need to know how soon we can arrange Nightfall's sale."

How had he shifted from her wedding dress to selling Nightfall so fast, and why couldn't her mind work like that? Clenching her jaw, Natasha pushed past him. All he cared about was erasing ties to Walkins from his life.

What else was he supposed to care about? She accepted Finn's choices, but her heart refused to listen. This wasn't some dumb script made for television movie. The hero returning to find what he missed. The girl he left behind became the woman he couldn't live without. No. This was real life. She was his uncle's widow. A piece of the past glued too far to too many memories.

Natasha grabbed her coat from the kitchen chair before rounding on his footsteps. Sucking in a breath, she tried to pretend the pain rolling through her was from exhaustion. Biting her lip, she looked for Mark. He knew about the stipulations Warren had in the will. Hell, as Warren's lawyer, Mark had crafted each one.

When Mark kept his mouth shut, Natasha rolled her eyes. *Coward!*

At least her oldest friend had the good sense to look away.

"You have to be here six months before you can sell." Gesturing to the stack on the table, Natasha frowned. "So, I'll happily sign the papers six months from now."

Finn's brows furrowed as he stepped towards her. "It has to be in my possession for six months, and I plan to hire someone to oversee the upkeep."

"You can't." Mark stepped into the kitchen.

"Finally," Nat muttered.

"Of course, I can. There is no need for me to be here for six months. I have a business to run." Finn started pulling papers off the stack.

She wanted to point out the finer points of the ranch being a business but elected to have Mark handle Finn's disbelief. Nodding her head towards Lauren, she gestured for them to take their leave.

Nightfall belonged to Finn. This wasn't her home. "I'm sorry. I shouldn't have intruded."

"Nat." Finn grabbed her wrist and immediately dropped it. "Sorry. I can't stay here."

Her skin burned from the brief touch. "No one is asking you to. Goodbye, Finn."

The words caught in her throat, but she wasn't going to let the first tears she spent after Warren's death be over a man who walked out of her life years ago.

She walked out Nightfall's door.

For once, Nat didn't look back.

Finn pushed his hand through his hair and stared at the closed front door. *What had her wedding dress looked like? Had she returned it?*

The answer to those questions wouldn't help the current situation. Their engagement was history. Ancient history. She'd canceled any plans she'd made long ago. *Without him*

His fingers tingled from their brief connection with Nat. When he saw her old, battered truck in the driveway, his heart leapt. It begged him to pull Nat into his arms, plead for her forgiveness, and implore her to stay with him forever. That wasn't possible, but his heart refused to listen.

"The will says clearly that *you* are required to run the ranch for six months before you can initiate the sale." Mark's flat statement brought Finn back to the current problem.

"I have my own company to run. Did my uncle conveniently forget that?"

"Sorry." Finn rubbed his face. Closing out Warren's estate shouldn't be easy, but he hadn't expected it to make him such an obnoxious jerk.

"Your uncle knew you had Reach, and that you would never give it up. However, he didn't want you to feel like he gave the ranch away without giving you an option first, either." Mark produced a pen from his pocket and began sifting through the documents.

"How do you know so much about Warren's will?"

"I wrote it." Mark set three pages aside before looking at Finn. "Warren's concern was protecting your and Natasha's interests."

"I read the will." Finn's stomach clenched. It wasn't a huge lie. He glanced at it several times, but his brain refused to accept the reality of Warren's loss. "It says nothing about me staying here."

"In his original will yes, however, he added an addendum to it a few months before he passed." Mark skimmed the document in his hand and circled a large section before handing it across the table.

Before my beneficiary may sell Nightfall Ranch, he must reside there for six months. Due to the nature of the beneficiary's successful business, I understand that he will be required to work part-time in California. However, he must reside within the grounds of Nightfall Ranch for at least three days a week or two, full weeks a month during this time before a sale can be initiated by my executor.

In the event my beneficiary does not wish to agree to these terms, all my assets shall be transferred to the executor to initiate the sale and donations of its proceeds to the previously outlined charities.

"There are only two options outlined here." Finn's brain spun as his mind grappled with the idea that Uncle Warren thought he might remain in Walkins for more than a week or two. He thought Warren understood that staying with Nat was not possible. Part of him had gone missing when they'd parted ways. He made do with the part of himself left and remade himself into a new man. If he stayed? Well, if Reach's board caught wind of any weakness, they'd use it against him. He'd already stayed to long.

The tapping of Mark's pen drilled through Finn's brain. "How am I supposed to live here?"

Shuffling the papers, Mark shrugged. "Warren wired the house for high-speed internet. He purchased a small video teleconference system, though you probably have access to better equipment. How do you operate the business when you are on a trip or vacation?"

"I don't take vacations, and my trips revolve around meetings."

Mark rolled his eyes. "Finn."

Why was his brain refusing to put the right words together? Blowing out a breath, Finn tried again. " I don't have experience with these types of operations."

"Perhaps it's time you learned." Mark pushed his chair back from the table, "There is another option."

"What?"

"You could attempt to sweet talk the executor into fudging your six-month requirement. That will require you to look past your own pain." Mark tipped his hat and turned towards the door.

"Wait." Finn stood. He didn't want to be alone, not yet. "How did you draw up legal documents?"

"It's one of the first things they teach you in law school." Mark scoffed.

"You're not a lawyer. Warren said that you're running your parents' dairy." The instant the words were out of his mouth, Finn regretted them.

"I passed the bar and keep my membership current. I took over the dairy after my father died. Mom couldn't do it all, but she didn't want to sell." Mark shrugged, "The dairy's been in our family for five generations. Sometimes, you adjust your dreams for those you love."

Was he challenging Finn? Pointing out he'd chosen his dreams over Nat's? That wasn't fair. She chose hers over his, too. "That's how dreams die."

"Only if the dream is weak. I practice three days a week for the locals. The dairy stays in the family, and Mom is enjoying some well-earned rest. You and I have different definitions of success, Finn."

"That doesn't mean my definition is bad." Finn's toes curled. Why was he defending his choice?

Mark tipped his hat, "Doesn't mean mine is wrong either. Have a good day, Finn."

The house's emptiness echoed around him. Finn was

alone. He should be used to it. Outside of the office and meetings, he was always alone in California.

His place looked more like a fancy hotel but not a home.

So why did the silence bother him now?

Nat. The answer was simple, but it didn't help.

Chapter Three

Finn fumed as he read the email from his Chief Financial Officer, Michael Henley. The board, Finn's board, was voting in three days to accept the recent offer from Smith, Anderson and Joveston International. No one could tell Finn what the hedge fund wanted to do with Reach. Finn didn't know if that was because of his anger, or if they hadn't bothered to ask.

Reach wasn't a company to him. It was his life. *His baby.* Finn spent two years couch hopping in strangers' living rooms, growing the firm from the first two engineers to a company that employed over three-hundred people. He couldn't lose it, and he didn't care how much money the investment firm was offering.

"Answer your phone," Finn growled as another board member's voicemail echoed in his ear. No one was responding to his email or texts.

Running a hand over his face, Finn dialed Michael again. He'd been with Reach longer than any other member. He had to understand.

"Finn." The rustling of papers punctuated Michael's

response. The man never stopped working, never stopped focusing on the next big thing, hence why he fit right in.

"How do I get the board to vote with me?" Finn paced back and forth through the house. If anyone could help him stop this, it was Michael. "How do I halt this sale?"

"Why on earth would you want to stop this? Have you seen your buyout amount, Finn? You will have enough to launch whatever next firm you want. Or never work another day in your life. This is the dream. It's why we all came on board."

Ice shot down his back. No. No. This wasn't the dream. It wasn't what he'd worked towards. "We started Reach to develop the best operating system."

"Right, so that someone would pay us a ridiculous amount of money for it." Michael sighed, "You should celebrate, Finn. We played the game, told the first few companies no, and now have an offer that is nearly quadruple the number initially offered."

"This isn't about the money." How could no one else see that?

Michael tapped his pencil against the desk. "Finn, maybe, if you were here and not off gallivanting in the middle of nowhere."

"I'm settling my uncle's estate."

"I know, but lawyers can do that. It's Wyoming. Seriously, why are you still there?"

The timing wasn't great, but Finn thought this was all wrapped up when he left. He convinced the board to say no to the three other deals. Why not this one, too? Staring at the kitchen, he swallowed the lump in his throat. He couldn't risk Reach for Warren's ranch. He'd have to find a way to make Natasha see that. "I'll be back by the end of the week."

"Finn," Michael's exasperated tone cut through the phone, "I don't know what you can bring to the table that will change this."

Finn didn't know either, but he had to try. He sacrificed everything for Reach. It terrified him to accept what life might look like without it.

"I need to run." Michael clicked off the phone without saying goodbye.

Spinning around the living room, Finn sighed at the blankets thrown over the couch. He'd been here almost a week and still hadn't made it upstairs. It was ridiculous.

Squaring his shoulders, Finn headed for the steps. After he convinced Nat to let him sell this place, he wasn't intending to return again. He doubted there was anything in his old room that he wanted, but Finn needed to see it, Enjoy the nostalgia, and then put this mess behind him.

The room's fresh scent hit him. The bed was made, and dust didn't coat his dresser. It looked just like it had the night he left. Finn laughed at the aging posters of bands that had broken up long ago. This room, Nightfall, Walkins, those old songs that filled all three spaces—they were his past.

Why did just the idea of packing this up make him want to scream?

Nat. Her name floated through his mind. Leaving meant saying goodbye to the memory of the woman he couldn't forget. Her life was here. She hadn't wanted to chase his tech dreams, though at this point, he could have funded hers. That had been his plan once upon a time. Get his dreams off the ground then make hers come true…

Finn flopped onto his bed. An object dug into the back of his head, and he groaned. Shifting, he hunted for the source under his pillow, and his heart stopped when he felt it's edges. The soft, velvet box could only be one thing.

The ring was shiny, but the diamond tiny. Finn remembered how proud he'd been the day he saved up enough money for this small declaration of love and devotion. Nat hadn't kept it. *Why would she?*

Hefting himself from the bed, Finn ran a hand through his

hair. He needed a haircut and a way out of Walkins. His heart couldn't take staying in the same town with Natasha, if she wasn't his partner. There would never be another for him, but their lives, their dreams, were too different. Not everyone received a happily ever after. However, he made one dream come true.

He wasn't giving that up now.

Finn pocketed the ring and closed his bedroom door. He didn't need more reasons to stay in Walkins. He couldn't see Nat today, couldn't handle angering her again. Tomorrow afternoon, he'd convince her to sign the papers and leave. Until then, he needed to find a way to stop the memories, fatigue, and anxiety from ruining him.

Passing through the kitchen, Finn paused. His old baking tins lay on top of the cabinet. Their light-blue tint brought a smile to his face. Standing on a chair, he lifted them down and coughed as years of dust wafted up to greet him. A laugh brewed in his belly at the forgotten cookware. Here was an area no one kept waiting for him.

Natasha hated anything to do with the oven. Warren had enjoyed the tasty treats Finn had produced but paid little attention to how Finn produced those results.

"Let's get you cleaned up," Finn murmured as the water ran over his fingers. When it was just the right temperature, he plugged the sink and set the pans in the center.

It was silly of her to check on him. Every time they'd seen each other, emotions escalated. Barbs were thrown and feelings hurt. Still, she'd promised Warren she'd help Finn, if he ever returned home. Of course, she'd agreed, not expecting to have to follow through.

Gripping the door handle, Natasha tried to settle all the emotions racing through her. *And the urge to run.*

She had done that once. It hadn't made her feel any better. The last thing she needed was a repeat performance. Finn was grieving and alone. Assuming he was still at Nightfall.

If he left? Nat swallowed. Finn didn't owe her an explanation of his whereabouts. If he wanted to let her sell Nightfall, he could send her an email—or just not fulfill the terms of the will. Still, she wanted to believe he would tell her before leaving Walkins.

Wondering about all of that did not solve her reasons for being here. So, she turned the key and opened the door. Step one complete. Now, to keep their tempers in check.

The sweet tang of sugar wafted towards her as soon as the door opened. How long had it been since that sweet smell hung in Nightfall Ranch? Natasha shivered with delight. If Finn had located his baking supplies, then he was more relaxed.

Kneading dough, or rolling out cookies, or attempting to craft the perfect pastry made her skin itch. The long list of ingredients. The knowledge that, if you didn't get it just right, it would fail in the oven. The tinge of burned smell that always seemed to follow. All those made her far too nervous a baker to enjoy anything.

But Finnegan? He was at his happiest in an apron and covered in ingredients. Trying out new recipes. Tossing the failures and starting over. The kitchen was his happy place.

Before he left, Nightfall always smelled like a bakery. He joked that baking relieved his stress and was healthier than booze. She'd never been able to replicate the homey scent for Warren, no matter how closely she followed any recipe. The slice-and-bake cookies she could buy at the store tasted fine but never brought the same spirit.

Finn was sprawled on the couch. One hand hung over the edge, touching the floor, and the other straddled the arm rest. A trail of drool dripping onto the pillow cemented the picture, and Natasha had to stifle a soft laugh. His neck was going to have more than a few things to say about that sleeping choice when he woke.

Why isn't he sleeping in his bed? She'd cleaned his room to ensure it was ready for him. *Had he even found his way upstairs?*

It didn't matter. He was a grown man. If he wanted to sleep on the couch, that was his choice. Despite the awkwardness of his position, he looked peaceful.

Once, she might have woken him with kisses. Instead, she laid a light blanket across him and left him to rest.

In the kitchen, a pile of cookware, spoons, whisks, and other baking instruments, whose names escaped her, soaked in the sink or stacked next to it, awaiting their turn with scalding water and soap. Sugar and flour coated most surfaces, and her shoes stuck as she made her way across the floor. Only exhaustion could have made him leave such a mess. He normally cringed at the sight of anything out of place.

Rolling up her sleeves, Natasha moved towards the sink. A little over an hour later, she sat back and looked at the kitchen's gleaming results. Perfect.

"I would have cleaned it, Nat. This home isn't your responsibility anymore. *I'm* not your responsibility."

The words hit her, and she flinched. She took a deep breath before turning to face the man a part of her still loved. "You need to rest and grieve, Finn. Friends help after the death of a loved one. A simple thank you works well in situations like this."

Finn nodded and then hung his head. "Sorry, Natasha. I appreciate the kindness. I just." Whatever words he wanted to say remained locked away. Moving towards the cabinet, he grabbed two mugs and started coffee as he motioned for her to take a seat at the clean table.

As the smell of coffee encircled the room, Natasha grabbed a sticky bun and savored the sweet tang of orange frosting. "California must not be too busy." Natasha winked at his confused expression. Holding up the bun, she laughed, "You haven't lost your touch."

"You didn't empty the trash." His tone was soft as he moved towards the pantry. Returning her wink, he slid the trashcan out of the cupboard. Burned baked goods crested to the top, and he smiled.

"I had to make two supply runs to the grocery store. I think the last time I baked may have been in this room." He sighed and looked around the kitchen. "No. I know the last time I baked was in here." Grief hung on his shoulders. He needed to slow down enough to heal. Why couldn't he see how drained he was? It wasn't just Warren's passing.

Nat had watched every Reach presentation. Finnegan was slowly disappearing. He'd lost weight and always looked tired, no matter how excited he was on stage. If he didn't stop? Well, his body would force it one day. That was likely the only thing that would work. After all, she learned long ago that she couldn't force him to slow down. Finn wouldn't be different now.

Handing her a cup, he sat down across from her. From his pocket, he produced a small box and set it in the center of the table. The velvet box contained yesterday's dreams and sat unopened between them.

"I found this the other night," Finn stated. Sliding the box across the table a nudge further, he asked, "Did you leave it in my bed to punish me? Force me to remember what I gave up? I guess I deserve that."

Part of her had wanted to punish him, but she never followed through with those ugly thoughts. It hurt that he considered her capable of such pettiness. "How could you think I would be so cruel?"

Finn shrugged before taking back the ring she'd loved. "I left, never called, never visited."

She didn't and couldn't offer any words. Lifting the cup to

her lips, she tried to will some of its warmth into her chilly fingers.

"Nat," Finn's whisper bore through her. "I told you it was yours."

Natasha barely controlled the snarky response her tongue ached to release. And the sadder, truthful one. *Why could or would I want it without him?*

Her father suggested pawning it. She'd refused and clung to the dream that Finn, one day, would want to give it back for far longer than she was comfortable remembering.

"I laid on it last night. Not exactly a subtle message."

Giving him a serious look, she reached for the ring. Their fingers brushed for only a second as he handed it over. Their old memories danced on the edge of her brain.

However, that wasn't the focus. Natasha stared at the small box and tried to remember putting it on the bed. Life was hectic in the last few weeks of Warren's life, the memories fuzzy and unreal.

"It wasn't worth much," Finn added.

It was worth everything. She caught those words before embarrassing herself. "Finn, I cleaned your old room two weeks before Warren died. Put fresh sheets on the bed and dusted, in case he let you know the severity of his disease. That box has sat on your nightstand since the night after you left. I put it there along with a note. However, the last month of Warren's life was difficult."

That was an understatement. The last month was hell. They'd argued about Finn. She cried about what was inevitable. Warren dealt with pain that medicine barely seemed to put a dent in. She hadn't slept, hadn't eaten, and hadn't done so many things.

"I guess it is possible I moved the box while dusting and forgot to put it back. I promise, I never meant to hurt you with any of this. Life goes on, time passes, and old wounds close." She took a steadying breath. *Even if they don't fully heal.*

Finn stood and pushed both hands through his dark hair. The motion mimicked Warren's so closely, her breath paused. He had raised Finn after his parents' deaths, but he favored the look of his father's side of the family.

Similarly, he was frustrated and angry with himself. Her ability to read his emotions remained intact, no doubt heightened by living with Warren for the last three years of his life.

"There was no note on my bed."

Thank goodness. She could recall every word of it. The shaking fingers she'd used to write it. The tears. That note was for Finnegan. The last thing she wanted was for Finn to see it.

Nat focused on the grooves worn on the old kitchen table, so he wouldn't see the emotions on her face. "I don't know where it went. The page was gone when I moved in after Warren's diagnosis. I suspect Warren read it and destroyed it to save me from embarrassment. It was simply the musings of a hurt girl, hardly worth reading."

Finn stood and walked out. Before her heart could react, he was back at the table—burdened by a large stack of documents. "I need to sell the ranch and close out the estate as fast as possible. Mark says you can say I met the eighty percent agreement mandated in the will without me residing here."

She pursed her lips. So much for not arguing. This was Warren's last gift. "I can."

"Great." Finn pulled out a pen and passed it towards her.

Anger spun through her belly. The audacity. First, he'd accused her of marrying his uncle for gain, then he'd ranted about an engagement ring, and now he was thrusting a pen in her face to sign away his uncle's gift. The shift of this conversation made her furious.

Flexing her fist, she tried to mentally count back from ten.

She made it to six

"I said I *could*, but I won't. Live here for six months, and you can do with Nightfall Ranch as you please. Leave, and you fail to meet the contract of the will and will not inherit. That was Warren's plan. Not mine. I will not honor his memory by signing away his gift."

"I can't stay here. Not with you," Finn's words died away as he stared at her in horror.

"Guessing you didn't mean to say that last line." Natasha bit her lip, refusing to acknowledge the hurt pounding through her. "I will keep my distance, and I am done being insulted by you. Be mad at Warren and be mad at yourself. However, I have done nothing but care for your family since you left."

"Nat, I didn't mean it. I have Reach and a life in California."

Holding up her hand, she glared at him. "I know. Your uncle wanted you here for six months, so you could rest." The words echoed off the walls. It wasn't her intention, but damn, it felt good to release some of her own frustration. "He never stopped worrying about you and the harm you were doing to yourself by refusing to do anything but work. Have you bothered to look at yourself, truly look at yourself, in the last few years, Finnegan? You look terrible. Your hair is thinning, you probably weigh at least twenty-five pounds less than you should, and your skin is sallow. I know, as Warren did, that Reach is the most important thing to you. Continue at your current pace, and you will be the richest man in the graveyard, with no one to visit your lonely and forgotten stone."

She grabbed her coat as she stormed past his slack-jawed silence.

"He never stopped loving you. Even from the grave, he's trying to show it. I will not tarnish his final blessing by letting you weasel your way out of it. You can't possibly hate me more than you already do, so what do I have to lose?" Slamming the door, she cringed as a few flower bottles crashed to the porch floor, but she didn't stop to pick them up.

Now they'd both slammed the other's door.

"I could never hate you, Nat." The words were hollow in the emptiness as the smell of coffee filled his nose. Staring at the immaculate kitchen, Finn hated how he tarnished her gift. Natasha was still the caring woman he'd grown up with and loved. His heart seized. She was still the woman he'd left.

Closing his eyes, Finn tried to take a deep breath, but his chest felt too tight. His body was tight and heartbroken. This was why he'd stayed away so long. Because this reckoning was what he deserved. And he'd known it would break him.

"How do I fix this?" Another question left unanswered. Slowly, he climbed the stairs. He needed a shower, clean clothes, and some way to apologize.

I'm jealous of a dead man. A man I loved and trusted.

Inside, Finn knew Warren didn't marry Nat to hurt him, but everything hurt at the moment. For the last decade, Finn's entire life had revolved around his company. Nothing had been allowed to interfere.

What do I have to show for it? He was worth millions, but those funds were largely tied up in stock options. Nightfall's sale would not earn him enough to sway the board. He needed to offset the most recent offer.

Finn's stomach clenched as he hit the top step. Even if he sold Nightfall today, it wouldn't be soon enough. He was throwing a Hail Mary sixty seconds after the game was over. Reach was gone. Warren was gone. Nat was gone, and he didn't know how to deal with tomorrow.

He climbed into the shower before it warmed, allowing the chilly water to cascade down his back as he shivered. Finn tasted salt as he laid his head against the shower wall. At least he could simply let them flow with the water. He didn't have the energy to lift his hands. Reality was brutal.

Without Reach, he didn't know who he was. And the longer he stayed in Walkins, the more he hated the man he'd become. "I wish I'd come sooner. Part of me wishes I never left."

Shivering as the hot water finally evaporated, he washed his body and stepped from the shower. Pausing in front of the mirror, he wiped away the fog and stared at himself. His hollow eyes traced his lean arms and flat stomach. His cheek bones were prominent and muddy exhaustion stains stood out under his eyes. His body lacked any of the muscles he'd had as a boy.

He looked tired and ill, just as Nat had pointed out.

Why didn't I notice? Why hadn't anyone in my company asked?

He knew the uncomfortable answer. His entire board looked over-worked. The 'price' of success, worn as a badge of honor. Wrapping a towel around his slender waist, he left the sorry image and tried to figure out how to apologize to Nat. As he slid jeans over his hips, he settled on baking some cookies. The sweets might sway Natasha to let him in the door, and perhaps he might strike on inspiration for the words during the hour it took to make them.

Chapter Four

Natasha fumbled with the pen between her lips and tried to keep a yawn at bay. Working from home was nice, but it would be too easy to slide onto a pillow and grab a nap. Exhaustion didn't mean there wasn't work to be done. The monthly accounts looked healthy, but the letters and numbers floated on the page before her.

I don't have time for this.

Closing her eyes, Nat gave herself a moment to focus. Not too long, otherwise she'd fall asleep. If anyone called, and she didn't answer because she was asleep? Well, that would not help her goal. Besides, the letters dancing was a problem she knew how to fix. A couple of deep breaths and rest for her brain before reengaging? She'd fought with the alphabet her entire life. She had it under control with the dyslexia techniques she'd learned. Unfortunately, exhaustion made it more difficult to deal with.

"You'd think it wouldn't matter now."

After all, exhaustion was her constant companion for these last few years. It wasn't fair that her brain never adjusted to the lack of sleep. At least, at home, she could wear comfortable sweatpants and sit cross-legged on the couch as little got accomplished.

She replayed the morning's argument with Finn a dozen times, and her emotions didn't improve much. Nat understood his anger at Warren. She expected it, given Warren's refusal to discuss the true nature of his diagnosis. They fought often. Her vacillating between begging Warren, to screaming at him, and then finally her acquiescing to his desires to keep it a secret. The problem was, she was the one dealing with the aftermath. Fighting with a ghost didn't accomplish much.

Picking up the business proposal again, Natasha tried to ignore the shifting lines. *No! Focus!*

She tossed the sheets across the table, glaring as they spilled across the floor. It wasn't fair. She needed to focus, and her brain refused.

Unless it was Finn.

That topic was front and center in her mind. She could recall today, the day he'd asked her to marry him, and the last night they were together.

That final night came easy. She sat in the fading light, alone, staring at her engagement ring. She slid it from her fingers as Finnegan's headlights disappeared. Accepting she wouldn't walk down the aisle had taken longer than she'd expected, when she laid the cheap piece of love in the cup holder of her truck.

That memory still haunted her, but the hurt, and most of the anger faded with time. Or she thought it had. Until Finn walked into Saddlers. Her left hand still held no diamond, but life had moved on in many other ways. *And yet, I'm still sitting in the living room, upset over Finn.*

Her phone rang, breaking through the memories' thick haze. Her finger hovered for a moment too long, and she sighed as the new voice mail icon appeared.

It would be so easy to close her eyes and take a nap, put off all the hard choices for the next hour or day. Instead, she gathered the papers and placed them neatly back on the table. Those were this evening's goals.

A list. That was what Nat needed. A way for the few neurons firing in her brain to focus all their energy. And as she checked items off, it would give her a little dopamine hit.

Make grocery list
    Get groceries
    Call Dad—don't argue about the company
    Pay electric bill

Her breath came a little easier with each thing she added to the paper. Things she could control. Items she could check off, on her own time.

Control. What a simple, precious word.

Caring for someone with a terminal disease robbed it from you. Routine issues became emergencies. Putting off a simple task for an hour might mean it didn't get done for weeks, if something happened. Pushing her hair out of her eyes, she added, "get hair cut" to the list. Her life was her own. A twinge of sadness pressed against her, but joy melted back against it.

She deserved to be happy. Warren was gone. Finn would be soon. Natasha Saddler had plans for herself and this town. *And it's okay to be angry, too. I'll show Finn how wrong he was that nothing happened here.*

Her belly growled. Time to check off grocery shopping. She could worry about a list later. Grabbing her purse, Natasha hummed a cheerful song as she headed for the door.

Maybe if I fake happy long enough, it will be real.

As she climbed the steps to her apartment, arms full of grocery sacks, she weighed the pros and cons of becoming a hermit. Or at least avoiding outings until Finn left town. Small towns did a lot of things well, but they were hot beds of gossip. More than one person stopped her to ask about Walkins's lost tech tycoon.

She gave the same bland answer each time. She'd seen him. He wasn't staying. Nothing else to note. More than one person responded with a raised brow to indicate they thought she was hiding something. No doubt, rumors would spin on their own.

A knock echoed as she slammed the last bag on the counter. Whoever it was, if they wanted to talk about her ex, she'd order them out. The last thing she was discussing was Finnegan Matus.

"It's open." The words were out before she considered the possibility she'd let in a vacuum salesperson or a host of missionaries.

"Nat?"

Finn. Damn. This was worse.

Next time, just send the missionaries.

Finn stood, unsure what to do as Nat put her groceries away without acknowledging him. At least she hadn't immediately thrown him out. When the last bag was empty, she folded her arms, leaned against the counter, and stared at him.

Now or never. He owed her an apology and so much more than the sweets he brought. The cookies seemed like such a poor offering. Swallowing the lump in his throat, Finn handed over the plate of cookies. "These are for you. I mean, I handed them to you, so of course you know they're yours. Listen, I wanted to apologize. I haven't been nice since I returned."

She pulled at the cookies' covering, and her lip tugged up. Not quite a smile, but at least she wasn't frowning. Grabbing a cookie, she met his gaze. A few crumbs tumbled down her bright yellow shirt as she continued to stare.

"I have been hateful and vindictive. I turned all my fury towards you. That's unfair." An unspoken thought made him nauseous. She'd been perfection. Handled everything with so much grace. And he'd been a dick with no restraint.

But Warren isn't here for me to yell at.

"It is unfair." He waited a moment, but when it was clear she wasn't going to add on, he continued, "I can't stay here for six months straight, Nat." Another thought that turned his stomach.

At least, not until the sale of my company is final.

"Why not let me sell it, Finn? Warren wanted you to rest, but he knew you probably wouldn't come."

Probably. She was offering him kindness. Warren hoped, but he died thinking Finn wouldn't return. And that was why he couldn't just sell it.

"Warren wanted me to have it. I didn't," the words caught in his throat, but Finn pushed on, "I feel like I owe it to him to stay. At least for a little while. I'm going to sell it after I finish the will's stated requirements."

Walkins wasn't home, but it could be a stopping point while he figured out his next steps. In response, he watched Nat open her mouth. No words came out. That was more than fair. He went from begging for her signature a few hours ago to saying he was staying for a bit.

The whiplash was understandable.

"What if I am here part time, until my company sells, and then I stay another six months to hammer out a new plan?" It was the first time he'd said the words sell and company out loud to anyone he wasn't trying to convince to turn away offers. They burned.

"Sell? Wait. What? Reach is being sold?"

"It might not sell." Those words were fantasy. The odds the ink was already drying on paperwork weren't a hundred percent, but they were far greater than zero. "It's something the board is considering. I can't really talk about it. Not legally allowed until the official announcements are made."

"I thought you owned Reach? If you don't want to sell, wouldn't you have a final say on that?" Her head tilted slightly, and despite the years of distance, she reached a comforting hand out to him.

He'd missed her.

What if she'd come with me when I left? What if I'd stayed? Would we be celebrating more than a decade of wedded bliss?

He squeezed her hand gently before lifting it away. Her touch felt too good. The last thing his heart could handle was reigniting the flames that once left him healing from scorch marks. "Starting a company is an enormous investment. I needed backers and investors. When I had little to offer, I offered stock. People take risks, hoping to one-day strike it rich when a company goes public or is purchased by a wealthy firm."

"When did the board decide to sell?" She had a cookie in each hand but her gaze on him.

"When the offers started dropping." He laughed, but there was no hint of humor. "Technically, the first vote is tomorrow. There is a whole procedure, and all of it boils down to Reach not being mine in a few months. The offers have been flowing in since the week before Uncle Warren passed."

His chest clenched. The company. Warren. The worst moments of his life were all tied into one, horrid blow.

"I was up late the night before Uncle Warren's funeral,

trying to convince at least three members of the board to ignore a deal. I overslept and."

"And missed your flight?"

"Yes." Finn blew out a breath. Fury, pain and regret poured everywhere. He had no one to blame except himself.

"I was so angry at the board and at myself. More offers have poured in since I've been here. They just keep coming. My board believes I came here to stall the process at this point."

Natasha nodded, "Did you?"

He deserved the brutal question.

"No. Or at least I don't think that's why I came. I needed to see—" He swallowed. He needed to see her. With everything falling apart, his soul had cried out for Nat. *For home.*

"Take a breath, Finn."

He followed her lead and continued, "I needed to see Walkins. I don't think I really believed Uncle Warren was gone until I got to Nightfall. It's so empty. Then, I learned he married you, and he hid his illness, and I feel like a giant ball of anger. I hate him and myself."

"I miss Warren," Nat offered. She shrugged before adding, "But I hate him right now, too. I hate that Warren never spoke to you about the true nature of his diagnosis. I hate that I was too cowardly to let you know because I was afraid of telling you about our marriage. I hate that Warren married me without telling you or giving you the option of objecting. And I hate him for dying."

Her eyes showed a brokenness, but no tears fell. "It's okay to be angry. It's okay to be hurt. All part of the grief process, even for a wife that wasn't in love with her husband."

Yes, you were.

He kept those words and the hurt they caused inside. "I should get going. Enjoy the cookies, and again, sorry for everything." He moved towards the door. He needed to collect himself and put the mixture of emotions he had about his ex in a nice mental box. Then lock it away in the deep recesses of his mind.

She followed him to the door.

"Finn," tears strained her voice, but it didn't wobble. "You are going to have to find a way to forgive yourself."

"I don't know that I deserve forgiveness."

Strong arms enveloped him. Nat's head only came to his shoulder, but her strength flowed into him. Her warmth and the memories of different times.

"We all deserve forgiveness."

Wrapping his arms around her, comfort seeped into his soul. He should pull away. Instead, he laid his head against the top of her hair. She smelled of lemon, strawberries, and home. Bending his head, he stared into her large gray eyes.

Home.

The feeling settled within him. "I missed you, Nat. I should have called, should have visited, and should have done so many things differently. I know it doesn't make up for anything, but I've missed you."

She smiled and tapped his cheek before stepping back. "I've missed you too. Well, mostly—the Finn that's been here the last few days can stay in California."

Laughing, Finn gave her a brief nod. "I'd prefer him to stay much farther away than that. I'm glad Warren had you."

"Thank you, Finn." The tension in her shoulders evaporated, and she embraced him one more time.

Her head tipped up, and Finn moved without thinking. As his lips met hers, part of him shifted, fixing ancient and long repressed wounds. The healing was short-lived as she pushed back against him. Heat flooded his cheeks as he ran a hand through his stiff hair and tried to find the words to repair this latest misstep.

"You're grieving and looking for comfort. It's fine." Her clipped tone sent ice through him as she opened the door. "Let me know if you need anything at the ranch."

He stood in the empty hallway, staring at her door, willing it to reopen. That was a dream he'd killed too many years ago. She was right. He needed comfort, but he doubted there was anyone else in the world who could provide it. He still loved her, would always love her, but their paths marched in different directions.

Chapter Five

NAT'S PHONE BUZZED, and her neck muscles screamed as her head popped towards her cell. "Damn it."

Her right hand grabbed the phone, and her left went to a knot at the base of her neck that never left. Rolling her head from side to side, she breathed, trying to force the tension to relax. To grant her some peace. When that didn't work, she glanced at the text message.

Free for a few hours.

Finn had sent her a few messages over the last week. Always to the point. A brief check in. And no mention of the kiss they shared. Nope, that topic was off limits. Not that either of them brought it up.

Her fingers slid towards her lips, and she purposefully pulled them away. He was grieving. She was grieving. It hadn't meant anything. They were comfortable with each other. Well, once upon a time, that was true. It was a slip. One neither of them was going to repeat.

Holding her thumb over the message, she looked at the emoji responses. The heart was not an option. Neither was the exclamation mark. The question was what she should put on for this conversation. He was likely letting her know they could meet to discuss the finalities he figured out.

I could just leave it on read, she thought. Answering Finn was difficult. Part of her wanted to ignore him completely, yet another wanted to check in on him. She told herself it was so she could complete her final debt to Warren, but a tiny sliver ached for something she would never have.

It was that tiny sliver that kept her answer short. Nothing Finn could possibly read into. Stalling was a healthy option. Finn informed her that, while he was working out Reach's sale, he planned to outline what his plan was with the ranch for the few months Warren's will required he stay. It was an important topic. She was the executor, and he was being proactive.

Hell, yesterday he'd texted as soon as his plane landed, asking for a meetup. But she'd found a reason to be busy. Twirling the phone through her fingers, she left the message unanswered. There were other things that needed done.

Her life didn't revolve around Finnegan.

The fall seed order was due. She needed to look through resumes for their new mechanic. The spreadsheets were always in need of updating. There was no shortage of tasks.

And one of those is closing out Nightfall Ranch.

Her sluggish brain refused to focus as her eyes wandered to her phone. Coffee, she decided, standing and purposefully leaving the phone at her desk. It wasn't like Finn needed an answer right away.

A quick glance at the ancient pot her father kept sent shivers down her back. Her dad didn't care what coffee tasted like, provided the caffeine kept him moving. The store pot often tasted of burned remnants from years of use. When her father finally sold his share of the store to her, she had plans for that pot's demise.

Elaborate ones. A mythical send off into the great beyond!

She'd suffered through one cup this morning and wasn't

having another. Besides, a quick walk might clear her cluttered mind.

"I'm going for coffee, Amanda," Natasha called without waiting for any response. Walking fast, she refrained from glancing back at her newest employee. Amanda was competent. She didn't have a ton of initiative, but she clocked her hours and did her job. That was enough.

Natasha paused at the corner and forced herself to move on. The store could run for twenty minutes without her. The bright day and light breeze refreshed her as she started towards Winen's Coffee and Chocolates. This was exactly what she needed.

"On your left," a runner called before they blew past her.

She wasn't the only one charmed by this beautiful, late spring day. In a few weeks, everyone would complain about the heat and storms, but no one could find fault with today's blue sky.

She opened the coffee shop door, savoring the first hints of roasted and ground beans as they mingled with sweet chocolates and baked muffins. She meandered towards the candy display case. Winen's made the best salted caramels west of the Mississippi River. With everything going on, she'd earned a treat. The only question was, did she buy one caramel or the half pound bag?

A hand laid across her shoulder, and she jumped, letting out a squeal. Brad Cross's coffee went flying, soaking his business suit. She grasped toward the counter for napkins to shove at the stain. Of course it would be Brad. Even Finn would have been better. Mr. Cross asked her out. A lot.

No was not an answer the man understood. Since Warren passed, Brad sought her out far too often. His smirk looked forced as he deftly moved her hands off his chest. "Good grief, Natasha. Why are you so jumpy?"

The quiet hum of the shop's conversations had ceased the moment she dumped his coffee on him. All eyes rested on them. A few whispers were already starting, but she kept her focus on the stocky man in front of her. "I'm sorry, Brad. I'll pay for dry cleaning and, of course, let me get you a new cup of coffee."

She glanced at Mandy and mouthed 'thanks' as her friend began to recreate Brad's drink. He snuck up on her, but the second apology slipped out, anyway, "Sorry, Brad."

"Please, Natasha, it's my fault," Brad interrupted as he shrugged out of his wet jacket. Not many people in town wore suits, other than to a funeral, but the insurance salesman always dressed to the nines.

He'd done well since coming back to Walkins. Not that he'd wanted to return, but shoulder injuries had ways of making those decisions for football players. Though more than one person whispered he never had the talent to make it professionally. Whatever the truth, he seemed perpetually prepared to make a sale these days. "I should know better than to sneak up on a woman fascinated by sweet display."

Yes, you should.

"Well, at least there is no place for your day to go but up." She offered a brief smile, then turned to the counter.

"Actually." Stepping up beside her, Brad placed his hand on her shoulder. *Again.*

Take the not-subtle hint. Nat shrugged it off, not caring for the frown crossing his face. She'd turned him down. Repeatedly.

He continued regardless. "I was hoping we might find time to talk about the final issues regarding Warren's estate and his policies."

All she'd wanted was a coffee and a walk outside. Now, she was stuck. The man could carry on exactly three conversations. Sales pitches, old football glory stories, and how great *he* was.

A lesson she'd learned from the one date they went on more than a decade ago.

There was no other insurance policy. Whatever game he was trying now was not funny. Natasha looked past him. She didn't have time for this. "The only policy Warren maintained was on the property, in case of damage. I have ensured those bills are covered until the estate is settled. I suggest you take any sales pitches to Finn." She stepped around Brad and grabbed her coffee from Mandy. It was past time to go.

Brad laid his credit card on the counter before she could pass Mandy the money. Fine. If the jerk was intent on paying for her caffeine, she wasn't going to stop him.

"Warren had a sizable life insurance policy, and you're the beneficiary." The whispered words came with his warm breath on her neck.

She purposefully stepped away from him. "You're mistaken. I oversaw Nightfall's finances for three years. There weren't any payments for a life insurance policy. Besides, no insurer would have covered a terminally ill client."

Her words were rude, but she was too exhausted to think through any estate issues today. And she was completely done with Brad.

Finn stepped through the door. She hated the excited uptick in her heartbeat. Next time, she was just drinking from the coffee pot at Saddler's. Ancient and burned coffee was better than subjecting herself to this.

Her gaze met Finn's, and he tilted his head. "You alright, Nat?"

She glanced towards Brad but said nothing. From the look in the Finn's eyes, she knew he understood. She wasn't the only one that could still read their ex.

Finn stepped towards her, and Brad stepped around her.

"Here's Finn. Why don't we all go to my office and have a nice chat?"

If she hadn't already spilled coffee across Brad's suit, Natasha might have slugged him.

"I have a meeting this morning." The lie slipped through

her lips as she moved towards the door. "Have your chat with Finn. He has some important decisions to make." Without waiting for a response, she headed out the door with her eyes trained on the ground to avoid any suggestion she was looking for another morning chat.

Finn made no move to stop her. At some point, they needed to go through the rest of Warren's things. But ever since his brief kiss, she had no control over the memories flooding her system. She also couldn't kill the hint of hope that maybe Finn would fall in love with Walkins and want to stay this time. It was a stupid reaction she needed to control before she spent time with him again.

Finn understood Nat's lack of eye contact. Brad made her uncomfortable. Years and distance stood between her and Finn, but he could still read her body language—now that he was no longer stewing in his own anger. He understood her desire to keep her distance. That didn't mean it didn't hurt. He saw her around town a few times over the last two weeks.

No matter where he saw her, she always left without speaking to him. Then again, she rebuffed his texts, too. He earned that. However, he couldn't move away from Winen's door until she was out of sight.

"How are you doing?" The man who'd made Nat uncomfortable stood in front of him, holding his hand out. Finn looked at it then moved around Brad to order coffee and a muffin without shaking hands. If he upset Nat, that was enough for Finn to want nothing to do with the idiot. That hint didn't seem to matter as Brad added, "I need to talk to you about your relationship with Natasha."

The stranger's casual tone stung. Finn didn't have a relationship with Natasha. He closed that door the day he drove out of Walkins. His heart fluttered as his brain pushed that desire away. Then he took a small step back as the man crowded his space. He'd seen this power play before. It rarely worked. "Sorry, who did you say you were?"

He knew the answer, but the clench of the man's teeth made it clear Finn's words had hit harder than they should. Brad wasn't the only one who could use power plays.

"Bradley Cross, Brad." He handed over an insurance salesman's business card.

A pushy one at that, great. Finn accepted it and raised an eyebrow without saying more.

"I played quarterback in high school." Brad frowned. Frustration clouded his features as Finn didn't respond.

He didn't remember the star quarterback, but he knew the type. They thought very highly of themselves. Finn bet Brad reminisced about high school long after walking across the graduation stage.

Finn turned to order, glaring as Brad attempted to pay for it. The young woman behind the counter seemed to be holding back a smirk as he pushed the card away and laid a ten-dollar bill on the counter.

Refusing to take the hint, Brad continued, "I handled your uncle's life insurance policy."

"I've been through the documents. There's no mention of a life insurance policy within his will." Making a deliberate show of looking around the man, Finn sipped his drink and made to leave.

"Natasha is the beneficiary of the policy," Brad followed Finn.

Those words halted his plans to walk out without bothering to acknowledge the man further. Damn. That would have been so satisfying. "If Nat is the beneficiary, then why has she not received the funds? My uncle has been gone for over two months. It was a natural death with no investigation. No need to prolong the payout. What gives?"

"There are some concerns regarding Natasha's intentions. Perhaps this conversation would be better at my office."

Finn's stomach tightened as he sipped his coffee. "Lead the way."

The walk to Brad's office didn't take long. The faded furniture didn't match the expensive suit. Interesting. Brad gestured for Finn to follow him into his office and immediately moved to his desk and started shuffling papers. "So, you weren't aware that Natasha is the recipient of your uncle's quarter-million-dollar life insurance policy?"

"No." Finn and Warren didn't discuss things like this. They'd talked about the horses Warren loved. The town, the people—except for Nat. Finn smirked as he raised his coffee cup. "Why did your company give a sick man such a large policy? Seems like a poor business decision to me."

Brad's lip twisted before he forced it into a tight smile. If the man ever played poker, it would be so easy to take him for everything. "The policy has been in place for over thirty years."

Likely since he took in an orphaned nephew.

He simply nodded and held his tongue.

Brad leaned across his desk, with his hands folded in a polite but powerful manner. "I probably shouldn't mention this. There are some concerns regarding releasing the funds to Natasha as the beneficiary."

Finn said nothing as he studied his surroundings. It might not be a good idea to freely flaunt wealth, and most people in this small town probably wouldn't know the price of Brad's brand name shirt ruined by a giant coffee stain. Instead, Finn leaned back, "Why is your company withholding her funds?"

A smile lit the right side of Brad's thin lips, but he quickly controlled it. "There are concerns Natasha married your uncle to benefit from this policy."

"You believe Natasha married my uncle, cared for him through three difficult years of terminal cancer, in order to benefit from a life insurance policy?" Finn let the words fall flat, though anger twisted through his belly. In his initial stage of grief, he railed against his uncle's widow, even before realizing it was Nat. Still, nothing about the woman before he left Walkins, or since his return, made him believe she could take advantage of anyone, let alone a close family friend. The idea was preposterous.

Holding out his hands in a sympathetic motion, Brad leaned towards Finn. "It was well known that your uncle's marriage to Natasha was not what one might call a love match."

"I was unaware insurance companies rated love levels for their policies. Though, I admit, my knowledge of the area is more in the *legal* arena."

Cocking his head to one side, the businessman shrugged. "Typically, we do not monitor such things, but occasionally, family is concerned. With sizeable sums, challenges sometimes occur. *If* you had such a concern, I *might* be in a position to ensure your wishes were known."

If you paid me, the unspoken words vibrated through the room. This was not the first time Finn sat across from someone who thought they had power over him. Twirling his empty coffee cup, Finn let the silence settle around them. Finally, keeping his anger in check, he drilled his gaze into the man sitting across from him. "Natasha and I were childhood sweethearts. I know her character well."

"*Knew* her character." Brad interrupted. His fingers tapped on the desk, and it was clear he knew the direction of the conversation and didn't like it. "You've been gone a long time."

And that didn't change a damn thing in this conversation. The cup's plastic lid popped off, and Finn forced himself to unclench his fist. Fighting with this man wouldn't help Nat. "Natasha Saddler is one of the kindest, most honest individuals I've met. She cared for her husband during the worst three years of his life. Clearly, Uncle Warren wanted her to be well-taken care of, since he promised Nightfall Ranch to me as a child."

Finn held up a hand and stood before Brad could argue.

"I do not need to strip Nat of my uncle's gift. Given that she is the recipient named on the policy, I see no reason that this discussion should be any of my business."

Without waiting for a reply, Finn headed for the door.

But he didn't leave without adding, "If Natasha should ask, I will tell her you offered to contest the money on my behalf—for a small payment."

Chapter Six

THE LENGTH of time she stood in front of the mirror studying her appearance drove Natasha mad. However, today had to be perfect. Everything she planned was riding on this meeting. Tucking a loose red curl behind her ear, Nat pursed her lips. Should she put on more than lipstick? She picked up the mascara tube for the umpteenth time and finally opened it. A couple of quick swipes couldn't hurt. She stepped back from the mirror.

She was leaving.

But is the business suit too much?

Nope. She would not second guess or, really, fifteenth guess her choice. She looked professional. A woman capable of taking charge. Her father never appreciated big city business types, but that was the attitude Saddler's needed to compete in today's online economy. Most of their competitors weren't shifting their business plans—yet. If Saddler's was one of the first to adjust, it would cement their company's legacy.

Take a deep breath, Natasha. It's just Dad.

She was the one for the job, even though her dad worried

about Natasha running the full operation. Her uncle left Walkins, so her dad knew what it was like to be the only Saddler in charge. Despite his long nights and fewer family vacations, Natasha loved Saddler's. It was a blessing, not a burden.

As retirement loomed, her dad bemoaned more and more that only his daughter returned home to Walkins after college. Her brothers 'were charmed by city life' and chose to remain in the Cheyenne area. If she listened to another diatribe on not burdening one child with the full workload of running the store, she might not contain her scream.

All her preparation was going to pay off. She strutted to the kitchen, and with her notes, practiced her speech once more before gathering her spreadsheets. Walking to her ancient truck, she shuddered as a crack of lightning raced through the black sky. Today's customer load was going to be exceptionally light.

More time to talk to Dad, then.

Amanda stood behind the counter looking bored. Natasha doubted any type of work would keep the young woman in Walkins much longer, but she wished Amanda looked pleased when people walked in.

"Good morning." Natasha kept her tone professional but focused an eye on the pink nail polish next to the cash register. "I think the incoming weather will keep most customers at home? I need to have a discussion with Mr. Saddler, and then, if the load is still light, I can relieve you if you'd rather head home."

Amanda slipped the polish into her pocket. "No. I need the paycheck. If it's light, I'll sweep and stock and," she paused for a moment as she looked around the quiet store, "manage."

"Alright." Nat nodded and started toward the office. The light waft of cigarette smoke touched Nat's nose before she reached the back hallway. She didn't bother to hide her frown as she opened the office door. Her father hurried to put the cigarette out.

Like that did any good.

"I could smell it in the hallway. Seriously Dad, if you are not concerned about your health, can you at least not break the law about smoking in a business? The county inspector could show up at any minute."

"The county inspector is more concerned with his golf game than issuing tickets." Her father folded his arms as he interrupted. "We've never been fined. I retire soon. Why change?"

This was the attitude that kept her father's business successful so far but limited its ability to grow. It was what she planned to change, and her father could not have given her a better opening for this conversation. "I'm glad you are looking forward to retirement. I wanted to talk to you about the plans I have for Saddler's, when I take full control."

Her father slipped his glasses off and red ran up his neck. He was already prepping for an argument. "Honey."

That was not an endearment she liked because some form of no always followed it. But not today. She laid a few graphs out. "As you can see, I've planned out Saddler's expansion. The family and friends' night was the first step. Ideally, this is a two-year plan, but I've got three-year and five-year time-lines, too. If the market shifts."

"You shouldn't have to do everything yourself. If I sell part of my share of the company, then you will still maintain over fifty percent of Saddler's. You'll have the controlling interest and have a partner to help you see this through. If your brothers were here, it might be different." Her dad pushed her documents away as he reached for her hands.

Natasha crossed her arms. This was a business meeting, and yes they were family, but this wasn't about that connection. "Is this because I struggle with letters and numbers?"

The question tumbled from her lips. That was not in the speech she'd planned. She couldn't suck the words back in.

Her father tilted his head. "Dyslexia. It is hardly a bad word. And it doesn't matter. You've done brilliantly. You graduated from college."

"Barely." Natasha snorted and hated the panic pressing against her chest. Her brothers were accomplished. Liam was a vet, and Caleb a lawyer. Standard, high-paying professions. She stood in the shadows of their academic achievements.

However, she knew the family business better than anyone. Here, she shinned.

"You have two degrees," he gestured at the wall. "They are worth every bit as much as any other. Who cares if you didn't graduate top of the class or with honors? Stop selling your academic accomplishments short. I've worked very hard to ensure you never felt Liam or Caleb had more because their brains are wired in what experts call the normal way."

"I know, but—"

"But nothing," her father roared. "You can't do everything Natasha, not because you struggle, occasionally, with letters or numbers. Because you are human. For the last three years, you have run yourself ragged taking care of a terminally ill man, while planning Saddler's expansion and building plans for additional services. I'm here now, but what about when I am gone? You're exhausted, and I'm terrified you're working yourself towards the grave."

Tears clouded her vision, but it was anger that tinged her voice. "I am *not* weak."

"That is the last word I would use to describe you. Life is more than work. Family and love make work worthwhile."

"I am a widow, or have you forgotten?" Her voice trembled slightly, and she hated the show of weakness. This was not how this meeting was supposed to go.

Her father pursed his lips. "I love you. What you did for Warren was amazing, but you used that marriage as another reason to hide from the world. To put off moving on with your life. Finnegan's—."

"This has nothing to do with Finn." Except that it did, and she hated herself for that. Ever since Finn decided Saddler's wasn't enough for him, that this life wasn't enough for him. She wanted to prove him wrong. To make this store, this town, something that he wished he'd been a part of. He'd just come home to soon.

Or not soon enough.

Her father's face relaxed with sympathy, and she feared pity. "Natasha."

"That dream died years ago." She couldn't let him continue. This was not why she was here.

"Did it? Or have you been waiting for him to return? He's back."

The soft words struck her hard, and she stood. "He didn't come for me though, did he?"

"His uncle is gone. You're the one he's here for, even if neither of you realize it yet."

"This conversation is over!" She scooped up her notes, cringing as some scattered across the floor. She was here to discuss the expansion. The conversation had gotten away from her. She needed to regroup.

This isn't about Finn. It's about Saddler's and Walkins and my future.

Her brain didn't even try to pretend that it believed her mental cries. Bending, she stuffed her papers into her bag and rushed for the door.

"You can't sell."

Pulling into the empty lot, Finn stared at the mix of green highlighted in the dark gray of the swirling clouds. That was a color one didn't see in San Francisco. The storm was going to be bad, and he hoped not to linger in it too long. The list of items he needed for Nightfall wasn't long. He could wait for tomorrow and head home.

Home. The word rolled through his brain. The last time he felt home was the tiny apartment he and Nat shared in college. The fridge leaked, the carpet was stained, and you could hear anything through the paper-thin walls. It was heaven.

Because I came home to Nat.

These thoughts weren't helping him get what he needed, and the clouds were going to open. Hopefully Saddler's sold umbrellas. Dashing to the front door, he hit the sidewalk just as the storm let loose.

"Managed to avoid the rain?" the bored, young woman barely looked up as she sat at the cash register while painting her nails.

"The back of my shirt's a little wet, but I'll survive. Do you sell umbrellas?"

"Aisle three end cap, but there aren't many. If you want a selection, you need to try the chain department store, or you could order online."

"It's a little late for those options." Finn pointed to the rain, making it impossible to see the parking lot. "I came for supplies. Is Natasha here?"

The cashier tilted her head towards the back office. Of course. Nat ran this place now. He headed back to the room he'd spent so much time in growing up. Before he reached the door, Nat's distressed voice echoed down the hall. "You can't sell."

She flung the door open with such force, Finn thought the hinges might fall off. Her face, the pink on her cheeks, darkened to crimson as her gaze met his.

"I just came for supplies." He'd interrupted whatever this was, but his brain had no words for what he'd accidentally walked in on. The list in his hand fluttered to the floor. Of course, this was why he used the note taking app on his phone.

But he hadn't wanted to see texts or news about Reach that he knew were flooding his notifications.

He bent to pick up the paper from where it had fluttered to the floor and head-butted Natasha. They both went sprawling unceremoniously next to each other. Then, without reason, Natasha laughed. A soft chuckle at first that grew into a full, bitter, belly laugh as she sat on the floor next to him. "Of course, you're here. Of course. Because that is just the way my life goes."

His chest clenched as she waved off his hand for help and stood on her own. "I'm sorry."

"It's fine." She pushed past him, racing for the exit.

His feet moved to follow before his brain could order him to stop. "Wait."

Large splats of rain blurred his vision as he followed her to her truck. Pulling open the side door proved difficult in the swirling wind, but he slid into the old beast. The cabin smelled of leather, perfume, and time. They'd had a lot of good times in this creaky beast.

Nat said nothing about his presence. At least she wasn't ordering him out.

The engine stalled, and Natasha struck her fist against the steering wheel, so the horn blurted an awful blast. Then, she laid her head against the wheel and looked at him with empty eyes. "If you were expecting a lift somewhere, today is not my day. Perhaps tomorrow."

"Why don't you let me try?" He waited for her to argue, but she tossed him the keys and opened the door before stepping into the downpour. He slid over the truck bench. She was drenched as she hauled herself into the passenger seat.

"I would have gotten out so you could slide across, Natasha." He waited for her to respond, but she leaned her head against the window, saying nothing.

It took four attempts, but the ancient truck finally turned over. Sliding the heat on and pointing the ducts towards Natasha, Finn tried to figure out his next move. After pulling out of Saddler's parking lot, he turned onto the highway and simply drove.

Chapter Seven

Silence and tension coated every edge of the truck. Conflicted emotions tied his tongue, and Nat seemed uninterested in the world around her. She hadn't fought with him when he took the wheel and made no suggestion regarding their destination. Pulling into the diner's empty parking lot, he let the engine idle for a few moments before turning it off. If she was against his choice, she'd have to say something.

The truck's windows fogged as the rain continued unabated. Maybe the sky was crying the tears Natasha seemed incapable of releasing.

Or maybe I just assume she should be crying.

Whatever blow up he witnessed was stressful enough. Nat used to cry at the drop of a hat. A dog food commercial could mist her eyes. Not now. Once more, Finn opened his mouth to initiate a conversation and then closed it.

The rain slowed to a steady drizzle and still she sat, unmoving, red hair matted against the windowpane. Without thinking, he laid a hand on her shoulder and she smiled slightly.

He had no illusions regarding her feelings for him. For a moment, though, he allowed himself to pretend she chose

him, rather than seeking comfort, and him being the only
option. For several minutes, he lightly stroked her arm and
listened to the rain beat across the old truck.

"Let me buy you a cup of coffee." He feared he might give
into the desire to pull her into his lap. She needed comfort. A
fact she was trying very hard to hide. Had anyone even
noticed? She'd taken care of Warren, Saddler's, everyone.

Even me, when I was such an ass.

Still, she continued to look out the window.

"If you don't want coffee, it could be an omelet." Nat
nodded, so he tried for a little humor. "Not the egg white
ones Mark eats now, though. A nice big one, with bacon,
covered in salsa and cheese."

A small laugh, barely loud enough to count, registered in
his soul as he opened the door and raced around to pull her
from the truck. Leading Natasha to a back booth, he motioned
for the waitress to bring a pot of coffee.

"I am not usually such a sulker." Her bottom lip quivered,
but she straightened her shoulders, meeting his gaze head on.
Then, she slid her soaked jacket off and laid it on the booth.

Her pink camisole clung to her thin body. Worry crossed
his brain, and it took him a few seconds to realize she was
waiting for him to say something. Despite the puffy eyes and
pink cheeks, she looked formidable.

Has she been eating since Uncle Warren died?

When she didn't continue, he added, "You have always
been strong, Nat. I would never make the mistake of accusing
you of sulking."

She closed her eyes, stifling a yawn. "Yes, well, today was
just a minor setback. One I'll rectify. Though running away
was a bad idea."

The rushed words died as the waitress laid the pot of
coffee and two mugs on the table. The older woman looked at
them, dutifully ignoring the signs of Natasha's distress.
"Food?"

His stomach leapt at the idea of a second breakfast, gurgling greedily. "I would like your largest omelet, provided it has cheese and bacon."

"You want anything, honey?"

"No, thank you, Doreen." Natasha smiled as the older woman dropped a pat on Nat's arm.

That sense of community was the main thing he missed in San Francisco. You could order anything at any time of the day. Everyone moved so fast. It was impossible to notice the everyday turmoil people suffered.

"I missed knowing everyone in town." Finn stared at the empty county highway outside the diner. The weather had abated and now a light mist covered the earth as far as he could see. A beat-up Cadillac blew past a large tractor, and he watched the farmer raise his hand in a friendly wave.

Natasha glanced out the window, then turned to the hot mug of coffee. Priorities in check. "It has its perks, but everyone knows your business too." Coffee splashed over the lip of her cup, as she added cream. "No doubt Amanda, our cashier, will inform everyone my father and I argued."

Blowing across the coffee, she sighed before adding, "Mark will call to check on me, and Lauren or Scarlett will drop by this evening."

The air quotes around 'drop by' made Finn laugh. He gave it a moment before asking, "Want to talk about it?"

Her lips pursed, and she pushed yet another loose curl behind her ear. "My father thinks it will be too much for me to run Saddler's alone. He wants to sell his share of the company, so I have a full-time partner. He thinks I should live my life, which I am pretty sure means marry and give him grandbabies."

Finn's stomach rolled at the idea of Nat meeting anyone at the altar, but he pushed the feelings aside. She deserved to be happy. He wanted, *needed*, her to be happy. "Typical."

Nat tapped her spoon on the table as she looked out the

window. "I explained I was a widow, and he expanded on his feelings regarding my marriage."

Maybe Finn should leave it along, but she needed to talk. Needed to let things out. "And Herb's feelings were not what you wanted to hear?"

"He thinks I put myself into a dormancy since," her words died away, and her gaze met his before she looked away, again. Perhaps she was as surprised as he that she provided any answer.

"Since I left."

Nat nodded but kept her gaze glued to the far side of the restaurant.

"Have you?

Time passed as the question hung between them. He didn't push her to answer, but his eyes roamed her face for hints. The bittersweet burn of coffee slid down her throat, but the empty cup delivered no words.

"You don't have to say anything," Finn whispered.

She refilled the coffee then looked at him. The small crow's feet outlining his eyes, and the soft laugh lines following his lips, showed how much time had passed. He wasn't staying. So what did she have to lose at this point?

Did you miss me?

She would not ask that question. If he said yes, and still returned to California, she'd always wonder if he might come home. If he said no, the bit of hope she kept would die for good. As much as Nat hated it, she wasn't ready to extinguish that ember either.

Looking around the desolate diner, Nat couldn't believe she was here. With Finn. It had taken years to rebuild her life following his abandonment. Without thinking, she simply let him come with her. Let him drive her here. Let him comfort her.

"Yes. Since you left, a small part of me has always been waiting for you to return. At first, that voice hoped you'd come home and beg me to go back in the car with you to our new home in California." She'd have done it. Gone with him. If he'd just asked her, rather than telling her their paths and goals were different. Shock crossed his face, but he didn't interrupt, so she pushed on, "I wanted you to beg me to take you back. On your knees and with such passion. You'd tell me you couldn't live without me." She watched his face, expecting horror, but he smiled instead.

Well, that is not a helpful response.

"There are days I wish I'd done that. Most days, if I am honest, and every day since I came home," his jaw clenched, and his eyes looked past her as she reached a hand out.

He gripped her chilly fingers before forcing a smile and letting her go. "It doesn't change that our lives are in different places now, but the idea will always live with me, too."

Are we in different places?

They were both living in Walkins. Natasha bit her lip as her brain reminded her heart that Finn's Walkins residency had a termination date.

"What about the larger part of you? What does that one want?"

At least that was a straightforward answer—mostly. "I want to run Saddler's and expand the warehouse into a full mechanic and repair shop for large equipment. Get us hooked up for large online orders and open an agricultural classroom in the back where kids can see the science behind the hard work. The added agricultural tourism could put Walkins on the map. People want to know where their food comes from, so we could focus on farm to table. There are a lot of restaurants partnering with businesses in those ways, too."

His left eyebrow raised. "That's *all* you want to do?"

She didn't like his emphasis on the word all. "Yes. That is what I am *going* to do."

"It would be easier with a partner."

"I don't need a partner." She wanted him to be her partner once and begged him to choose Saddler's and her dream. Now, she was determined to do it on her own. She was more than the woman dumped by the town tech genius.

"People are leaving Walkins," Natasha gestured at the highway. "That's a one-way path out."

"People have been leaving this tiny town since long before you and I were born. There is nothing here for anyone not interested in running a ranch or a farm."

"I know!" The words were too loud and the couple of old men sitting at the counter turned to look at her. He wasn't wrong. That was the problem. The one she was going to fix. Gathering herself, she took a deep breath. "I know all the reasons people leave, but what if there were other jobs here for those who wanted to stay? There is a ton of unused land, and our economy could support several business ventures."

"The town wasn't interested when I tried." Finn pulled at the collar of his shirt, "Although, maybe they just weren't interested in me."

There was so much more to the story than that. It hadn't felt like it, but with age came a wisdom people didn't always want. "Finn, we were at the height of a recession. People were focused on not losing their ranches. It wasn't you."

The recession was one of the reasons she wanted to grow the area, give it some cushion when another hit.

"Felt like it." His gaze studied the coffee mug as, if he watched it long enough, it might do something. Focusing on something, so he didn't have to acknowledge the hurt.

"Oh, Finn." Nat reached her hands towards him again and then pulled back. She wanted to shake him. He founded a multimillion-dollar tech company. How could he not see how proud everyone was of him? Sure, they wished he'd come home to visit, but the town was still proud of Finn's accomplishments.

He continued, "We're talking about present day Walkins, though. How do you know all the reasons people leave?"

"I've surveyed the last twenty graduating classes. About fifty percent of those who left want out of Walkins, or even out of the state of Wyoming. The rest felt they had to leave to support themselves." Each time she received a response that said they wanted to stay but couldn't afford to, Nat broke a little more. Those cuts were the reason she wanted this to work. Proving Saddler's was just as viable as his company was a nice added bonus.

"I wasn't part of that survey." He frowned before his eyes shifted to the highway.

"I emailed your company but received no response. You're categorized in the survey as part of the roughly three percent I couldn't contact, or who chose not to participate." She'd thought of calling him. In the end, she sent the simple email. It probably slipped into a spam filter as soon as it hit the box.

"I would have told you that I couldn't accomplish my goals in Wyoming. You could have easily filled it for me."

"I know. I could've supplied your answers, but that wouldn't have been fair. I'll update it when I get home, if you want, and consider this an interview in lieu of the email response." His numbers wouldn't change the percentages, but if he wanted included, she'd do it.

"Please do." He grinned.

Finn's smile warmed her heart. Such a small thing. It didn't change her metrics, but when he hadn't responded, it ripped another, small wound in her heart. He hadn't been avoiding her. It was nice to know, though it didn't help burst the bubble of hope she carried.

"For what it's worth, I agree with you but also with your father."

"You agree with my father?" The eyes of the diner turned towards her, again. The gossip mill was going to have a blast.

Finn raised his hands in defense. "Walkins has the potential to be more than ranches, farms and a tiny downtown. *But* you cannot do it all on your own without killing yourself."

"Watch me!" No one was going to tell her she couldn't.

Reaching for her hands, Finn squeezed them. "What will you do if he sells part of his interest in Saddler's?"

Staring at the chipped, red polish on her fingers as they sat in his hands, Natasha tried to determine how much to say. She'd had a backup plan for years. Her brother sat up a limited liability company that did not appear to have any ties to her. Tricking her father into selling the company to her without realizing it wasn't ideal, but she hated the idea of anyone other than family owning a part of Saddler's.

"I'll think of something." This time, she broke their connection.

Whatever reply Finn might offer failed to materialize as Doreen laid a foot-long platter of eggs smothered in chili in front of him. Then, she started a kitchen timer and sat it on the end of the table.

"What the?" Finn stared at the breakfast monstrosity in horror.

"The largest omelet they make is the Walkins Chili Challenge. That is ten eggs, a quarter pound of sausage and bacon, covered in Doreen's award-winning chili."

"I'm afraid to ask about the timer," Finn stated before lifting the first bite to his mouth. His eyes closed, and he smiled. Doreen's chili had that effect on everyone.

"*That is amazing.*" He scooped up another big bite.

"You have one hour to eat it, and it's free. Otherwise, you owe them thirty dollars, and your picture goes on the wall with the other losers."

He couldn't stop the groan from leaving his lips if he wanted. Finn should have given up twenty bites ago. Hell, fifty bites ago. The omelet had well and truly beaten him. "If I ever see another egg, I may toss my cookies."

"You love eggs. I give it three days before you're eating those words. Besides," Nat twirled the small kitchen timer, "you still have three minutes to go."

Nope. That was not going to happen. He reached for the timer, ignoring the heat racing up his arm as their fingers touched for a millisecond. Forcing it towards its destination, he leaned back and waited for Doreen. Hopefully, they could take his picture in the booth because there was no way he was moving any time soon.

"You're looking a little green," Natasha laughed, but worry tinged the playful tone.

Rubbing his aching belly, Finn opened one eye and winked at her without speaking a word. He feared his stomach might rebel, and he had no intention of embarrassing himself further. Doreen's husky voice trailed across the table, "As tries go, this is pretty sad. Four eggs left."

The sarcastic voice hit him, but Finn took no offense. "Guilty, Ms. Doreen. I failed miserably. Any chance you can take my picture while I am reclining in this booth?"

She raised her phone, "Smile."

It was going to look terrible, but at least it would fit in with the others. Time passed, but not enough, before Nat stood. "I need to get back to the office. Can you make it to the truck?"

Contemplating the ruin of his stomach, Finn figured he was likely to make it without losing the very heavy second breakfast. Standing gently, he stated, "I just need to pay the bill."

"Already took care of it."

"I was supposed to buy you a cup of coffee." This was not the plan. He was supposed to take care of her. Comfort her.

Not the other way around. At least the sorry attempt at the omelet challenge entertained her.

"You can get the next one."

"Next one?" His voice shook a little as his heart jumped, but she didn't seem to notice. The next one was going to be somewhere nicer than the diner. A real get together, not a you-have-no-other-choice moment.

Opening the diner's door, Natasha motioned for him to hurry. "Sure, friends go to dinner every once in a while. They also never tell others they saw them running out of a business meeting in tears."

"You weren't crying."

"Figure of speech." She flashed him a brilliant smile.

Friend. *Friend.* How that word stung. They could hardly be any more than friends. After he completed the terms of Warren's will, he'd head back to California.

My ties to California end with the sale of Reach.

The mental thought brought his feet to a standstill. Staring at the highway, the one way out, the way he'd left so many years ago. He wasn't required to take it again. Not unless he wanted to. He could stay. Staying wasn't an option.

But it is.

"If you're planning on vomiting, I would appreciate it if you did it before getting in the truck." Natasha was standing on the door of the truck looking over the top of the cab. He wanted her doing that more often while waiting for him. Like she used to.

"I promise not to hurl while in the confines of your precious truck." Crossing an X over his heart, Finn prayed that was a promise he could keep. Wrenching open the door, he smiled as she stuck the keys into the ignition. The engine coughed repeatedly before finally rolling over. "This thing is older than us, Nat."

Lovingly patting the cracked dashboard, she purred, "It still has a lot of miles left."

Focusing on the sounds coming from under the hood, now clear without the constant beat of rain, he didn't have the same confidence. Finn suspected the old beast was within fifty miles of its last journey. He moved to adjust the radio to drown out the rattling sounds, he frowned as Natasha pushed his hand away. "Busted?"

"Temporarily out of commission," she chimed.

Squinting at the dial, Finn raised an eyebrow. "How long's it been out of commission?"

"About two years."

While she was married to Warren. Nat was tough. That didn't mean she had to sacrifice everything for others. "Do you want a new car? I know the estate technically cannot be finalized until I finish the six-month requirement, but surely we can see that your portion is allocated sooner. I am sure Warren wouldn't mind me ensuring his widow had reliable transportation."

Her jaw clenched, and the whites of her knuckles highlighted against the steering wheel. "I am more than capable of purchasing a new vehicle *when* it is necessary."

The clipped words slapped him. Trying to repair the damage, Finn offered, "I didn't mean to offend you. I know the last three years you focused on Warren. The executor position is more than enough for a vehicle that doesn't sound like it is coughing down the road."

"My savings account is exceptionally healthy. Thank you for your concern."

Electing to drop the uncomfortable topic, Finn focused on the empty fields. "Could Nightfall be used as something other than a horse ranch?" He wasn't sure what he meant. The question was clinging to him. He liked horses, but they weren't his passion.

Chewing on her bottom lip, Natasha's eyes never left the road. "What do you have in mind?"

What do I have in mind?

She'd given him honesty today. He owed her the same. "I'm not sure. I just blurted the words out."

She didn't react. Didn't ask questions. They drove the rest of the way to Saddler's in silence. They bridged a gap today, but Finn feared a gulf still stood between them. He wasn't sure how to cross it, or if she would let him.

"Thanks for the company," Natasha gave him a smile and then stopped. "If you are interested in looking at other options for Nightfall, Mark can help with property law. He knows most of the city council, so he can give you a feel for their reactions."

He watched her walk into the store, trying to catch his breath. In another life, he'd chosen to stay, or taken her with him, but those fantasies didn't matter. Maybe they could be friends. It wasn't until he got home that he realized he'd forgotten all about the supplies.

Chapter Eight

T URNING the key in her ignition, Natasha cursed as the final bell rang. She driven here on instinct, but if her truck hadn't refused to start, she'd have left. There was no need to drop her problems and issues on a friend.

Then what are friends for?

Nat solved her problems. She helped others out. That was how this went.

"Stupid truck!" She hit the steering wheel before hopping out of the car. May as well see if Lauren could give the old truck a jump.

Children streamed out the school's front door before running to parent's outstretched hands and the promise of an afternoon snack. The red brick building had changed little since she walked its long halls. Her fingers traced the rows of hooks, and her eyes floated across the mismatched canvases of children's artwork. Laughing as she stepped on a fallen piece of macaroni, she gazed at the remains of pasta art along Lauren's door.

Natasha used to dream of sending her children here. Of walking them to school, hanging art on her refrigerator, helping with homework. A lump caught in her throat.

Natasha had planned on Finn helping with the homework, but those dreams turned to dust when he left.

"Looking at our pasta people?" Lauren asked as she stuck her head out.

"They appear to be mostly falling pasta people." Natasha pulled a piece of pasta off the bottom of her shoe and chucked it into a trashcan. There weren't going to be any pasta people to hang on her fridge, but if she could help others meet their dreams of raising families in Walkins, then maybe that would fill a bit of the empty hole in her soul.

Natasha grabbed baby food jars full of discolored water and followed her friend to the small workroom. "It looks like a color bomb went off in here."

Lauren smiled at the disaster. "Kindergarteners and finger paint will destroy a room in no time." She wiped away the smears and dumped her paint brushes in the sink. "You didn't come to clean up after a colorful day. What's on your mind?"

"I want Finn to leave." The selfish statement hung in the workroom.

"Have you asked him to?"

"Of course not."

"Offered to fudge his six-month requirement at Nightfall?" Lauren raised a brow as she looked over her shoulder.

"No," Natasha whispered, though she'd come close more than once. It was fear that he'd jump at the opportunity that kept her lips from offering. Still, he saw her several times since their impromptu breakfast date a week ago. Each time he asked after her. Chatted about everything and nothing, and never asked to skirt the requirement.

And he always ends the talk with the offer of coffee or lunch.

And she was losing the will to find other things to fill her schedule. After wanting him home for so long, she wanted him gone.

If he doesn't leave, I am going to beg him to stay.

Swallowing, she looked at her friend. "He's not asked to be let out of the will's requirement again. He's been flying back and forth between here and California." When Finn was in town, her skin itched with need, longing, and fear. Every time she turned a corner, Natasha was terrified she'd bump into her ex. And heartbroken when she didn't. It was a dichotomy she did not understand or need.

"He's been," she hesitated for a moment before settling on "friendly."

Lauren bobbed her head. Her short blonde hair stuck out in several directions. Paint splatters covered Lauren's shirt and a few blue fingerprints were on the bottom. She looked like she'd stepped from the pages of a children's book. Her eyes hinted at a worldliness she kept buried. "You still care for him. There is no shame in that, Natasha."

She opened her mouth to deny it but then closed it. "He abandoned me."

Lauren grabbed her hand, squeezing lightly before grabbing up the tray of paint and brushes and water cups. She led them back towards her room while somehow balancing everything. "*Abandoned*. That is quite the charge."

"He didn't ask me to come, not really. He said he needed to go to California. It was clear that there was no expectation I'd come. When I asked about Saddler's, reminded him that he'd promised to help me expand it; that it was my dream. He said that I didn't believe in him. I argued that we should have more savings. A plan that involved more than riding off into the sunset." The words flew from her lips, like a dam had broken. "Finn said he was tired of this town not believing in him. Lumped me in with the rest and told me I could keep my engagement ring. Then, he left."

She fingered her left hand, a habit she'd never managed to break after she deposited the tiny engagement ring in Finn's room. Her wedding dress hung in the closet at her parents' house for almost six years. After she donated the dress, she cried the entire way home.

"We were so young and inexperienced. If I'd packed my bags that night and ran away with him, I don't know what would have happened. In my mind, I can pretend that it would have been a perfect mistake. That we'd have imploded and broken up."

"Or pretend that it would have been a loving, lasting union," Lauren added.

Biting her lip, Natasha nodded. "In those first few months, even years, it was easy to pretend we would have hated each other with time. That the stress of building Reach and being away from home would destroy us. If I am honest, though?"

"If you're honest, you might have struggled, but you would be looking forward to your ten-year anniversary now." Lauren finished in a soothing tone.

Rather than travel down that worn path, she transitioned, "I've always loved home, but if he'd given me more than ten minutes to decide, I would have come. I went out there after he left, went to Reach, but I wasn't able to get past the front desk. Leaving Walkins and Saddler's would have hurt, but losing Finn was like losing half of myself. It's easier to pretend I had a real chance to say no thanks when he's not here."

Lauren leaned against her clean desk and pressed, "Ever plotted a way to make him stay if he came home? Or take you with him when he left?"

Sliding out of her chair, Natasha forced a smile, "Several times a day, at least in the last few weeks. So, now you can tell me I am pathetic and take me for a drink."

"I think you have the chance to find out the answer to what if? But the answer may not be happily ever after." Her friend's dark eyes bored through her.

"Not responding is also an option." She looked at the

desks. She'd dated after Finn left. No one made her feel like he had. No one came close.

"It is. Provided you will not spend the rest of your life asking yourself what if. Life is to short for that." Lauren grabbed her purse.

"So, no simple answer." Nat stuck her tongue out.

"Life has no simple answers. You know that better than most. Now, you owe me a cola for my free advice." Lauren winked before adding, "And I owe you a margarita for your sorrows and hopes."

The sun was just starting its rise over the edge of the horizon as Finn stepped onto the back porch. The stillness sent chills through his body. There should be horses neighing, people working, and the general clatter of ranch life. Even this early in the morning.

It was wrong. Tomblike.

His phone buzzed. Lifting it from his pocket, Finn wasn't surprised to see Michael's name. "It's sunrise here in Wyoming. You are an hour behind me."

"And yet I knew you'd be awake."

Touché.

"Finn, I have our next company." Michael was breathless as he shouted into the phone.

It was too early to discuss this. Too early and too late. Finn had ideas. Ideas that had started cementing the moment he'd realized there was no reason to leave. "Michael?"

"No. Don't interrupt. I know you're mad about Reach, Finn. I get it. I really do, but this is going to be even bigger." Michael let out a howl, and Finn knew he was punching the air. "It's *so* big."

"Michael."

He continued without letting Finn get another word in.

"I've already secured us interviews with the team at Stix. It's a formality. We are in. Their artificial intelligence products are going to change the world. We'll be rich!"

"We're already rich," Finn sighed. He had more money than he could spend in this lifetime, and he didn't want to join another startup. He wanted something that was his—something no one could take from him.

Looking across the open fields, his heart soared. He wasn't punching the air, but that didn't mean he wasn't excited. This land had so much potential.

"I'm talking billionaire status, Finn." Michael clicked his pen and sucked in a breath. "With the right investments, our buyout portfolios will reach that in a few years if the market holds."

What was the point of constantly building and selling a company? So you could have even more money you could never spend?

Reach was gone. It didn't matter that Finn poured the last twelve years into the company. It was still just a company to everyone else. An asset to be divided and profited from.

"Nah, man. This company is going stratospheric. A unicorn!"

"We've heard that about other startups, Michael." Finn let out a deep breath. He wasn't joining the company, but he liked Michael. Jumping from Reach to another company was fine, but he needed to think it through. So many companies were called unicorns until the word lost all meaning.

As the sun finally crested the flatlands of Warren's ranch, Finn felt a subtle rebirth. Nightfall was going to be a ranch with another purpose. Part ranch, part research facility to develop apps and tech to aid agriculture. He could keep a few animals and plant small amounts of sugar beets and wheat to hone the apps' capabilities.

If Natasha was right, a sizeable portion of Walkins wanted to remain here. Software engineers could build apps. The knowledge to make farms and ranches successful was locked in the minds of their owners and passed down to their children. He could hire the consultants from the local population. Teach the high school kids coding. The ideas were limitless.

This was going to work. And be his. All his.

"Just listen to the pitch. I know you're sore, but the pitch."

"I've already got something lined up, Michael." His heart sang as he watched the sunbeams hit the field.

"Really? Does it have the potential Stix does? If so, I might want to throw my hat in the ring. I mean, I could be persuaded." And that right there was the reason Finn couldn't join Michael at Stix. It wasn't the mission or the purpose of the company, just the dollar signs.

Finn learned from watching startups rise and fall that there were two varieties of the Silicon Valley types. Those that had enough, and those that would never have enough. If they had enough, they could be the vehicle to chase any dream. The latter would never find satisfaction, no matter the amount in their bank account.

His plan had so much potential, but not the kind Michael was talking about. "I'm going to start an agriculture software firm designing products to aid farmers and ranchers."

"No way that makes you a billionaire."

Finn laughed. He never planned to be a billionaire. Whatever he did to make one of the people he considered a friend think that was his primary goal was something he never wanted to be again. "I do not know how much it will make me. There is more money in agriculture than you know. What I know is, no matter the profit level, this venture helps the town I grew up in. My home."

This was the right choice. The sunrise touching the edges of the field seemed to sing with joy. Like letting them come out was a contract he signed. A proof to the land that he was its caretaker.

"Do you mind if I see if Anna wants your interview at

Stix?" Michael's voice was distant, already plotting his next move. A reminder that this wasn't personal. Only Finn had seen Reach as his baby. Only he cared about it at a deep level.

"Of course, and good luck, Michael." It didn't surprise Finn when Michael clicked off the call without a goodbye. Smiling, Finn stared at Nightfall. He was home. To stay. It felt right. *Nat.*

He needed her in his life. It was selfish, and if all she ever offered him was friendship, that would be enough. There was no way he was losing her again.

Natasha stared at the screen of her computer and silently swore before checking her phone. *Nothing.*

She came to Nightfall, hoping the tech guru could fix the nightmare that kept scrolling across her screen. This was the last thing she needed. Finn hadn't responded to her text, but she'd showed up any way. She logged into her laptop this morning to a text box ordering her to deposit twenty-thousand dollars of bitcoin into a foreign bank account. The timer on the pop-up was rolling down. Second by second.

She could pay it. May have to if Finn didn't walk in from wherever he was!

This wasn't his fault. Nope. It was hers. Somehow she'd left a backdoor into her system that a hacker had exploited, and now all Saddler's records were at risk.

And Nightfall's.

In order to make her life easier, she combined everything years ago. Co-mingling her responsibilities to save time.

And it may have gotten me hacked on a personal level.

This was stupid. And costly and just so fucking unfair. The first tear hit her cheek, and Natasha ran a finger through the wet trail it let behind. After all this time, all this energy, a tear. A single tear.

The tension bubbling in her chest that was her permanent companion over the past few years exploded. And with it, every tear she'd held back for so damn long.

"Nat?" Finn's voice called from the front door. "You here? That's great. I will warn you I've been for a run so—"

His words stopped as he stood at the kitchen entrance.

She should say something. Do something, but after refusing to let her cry, her body seemed incapable of doing anything else.

"What's wrong?" He was at the kitchen table in a second, sliding into the chair across from her. "Nat. Whatever it is, I'll fix it. But, honey, tell me what is going on."

Honey. The nickname slid off his lips so easily. Part of her ached to fold herself into his lap. Let him hold her, but she had come here with a purpose. What was the point of returning to good graces with your tech ex, if he couldn't fix a hacking issue for you?

Still, no words came as embarrassment competed with the tears flooding her cheeks. As the initial seconds of silence turned into minutes, and her tears continued to stream. Finally, she turned the screen away from her and gestured to it. Cocking his head to the left, she almost smiled at the familiar gesture. Once upon a time, she joked that his teachers knew when he was paying attention, or daydreaming, simply by the tilt of his head.

"May I?"

"That's why I'm here." If anyone could fix this electronic mess, it was Finn.

His fingers flew across the keys, doing god knew what. For the first time since Nat saw the message, she managed a full, relaxing breath.

"When did they send the ransomware?"

"I got this notice when I logged in this morning. I do not know how to get that much cryptocurrency." She could have used her phone to search, but all her brain cells had short-circuited when that window came up.

"There are exchanges, but that isn't the first problem to fix." He glanced at her across the screen. "Everything on here, I assume?"

"Yes. And it's affecting the store, too. Dad is on a fishing trip, thank goodness. Is there any way to fix this?" If he knew, this was going to be one more leverage point against her and owning the store outright.

Finn stood and went to the fridge. He pulled two beers out, opened them, and passed one over to her. It was too early for beer, but she didn't care.

The first swig was sweet as the hops hovered on her tongue. The second tasted even better. And the tears were finally drying up. With any luck, he could strike a few more keys and whisk this problem away.

"It's too early for me to tell what kind of hack this is. They can range from simple, to impossibly sophisticated, with no other option than to pay."

"Finn, you are a tech genius."

"You flatter me." He winked as he tipped the beer back.

She rolled her eyes, then pointed to the computer. "You clicked more than a handful of keys. I watched you do some questionable stuff when you were learning coding and hacking skills in high school and college. What kind of attack do you think this is?"

"Nat, I just started." His eyes flicked to the floor.

No. No. No. They'd lived together for years. And been apart less than forty-eight hours at any one point until he left. She knew his tells. This was the sophisticated attack. The kind that required payment.

She could pay it. The hit would hurt, but Saddler's could weather the financial burden. But there was no way to accomplish it without her father finding out.

"My father will use this as proof that I can't run Saddler's on my own." Natasha hated the moan. Hated the despair and the tightness in her throat. The tears were streaming again. She lost any will to do more than lay her head on the table and let the sobs take over. It didn't matter if Finn witnessed one more breakdown. She was too exhausted to pretend everything was fine.

Finn started towards her, then stopped. He did not know how to respond. She'd kept him at a distance since their discussion at the diner. Sure, they met up here and there to handle things at Nightfall, but Lauren was always with her. This was more than an argument with her father or worry about Saddler's.

Her running to him with a computer problem made sense. Nat's inability to control the sobs racking her small body broke his heart. This was a woman who'd finally lost the ability to hide her burdens.

"This could happen to anyone, honey." There was the endearment again. He hadn't meant to use it either time, but it just came so naturally. She was blaming herself for what was an unfortunate cost of doing business in the twenty-first century.

He set his beer on the table and pulled her up into his arms. The woman needed comfort.

She collapsed into him, hiccupping unintelligible sounds that were probably failed attempts to stop the pouring tears.

Finn ran a hand along her back. "I employ an entire team to hack my software and then fix the breaks when they find them. Even that level of preparation hasn't stopped two very skilled attacks, one that made international headlines."

"Well… I shouldn't… have let… it happen," she let out the words between sniffles.

"Why? What makes you so special?" Maybe that wasn't a fair question, but she couldn't do everything. Natasha forced him to see how drained he was and how much he needed a break. It was his turn to drive the same message home.

"Excuse me." Her head snapped up. She stepped out of his arms and crossed hers. The wall that had fallen between them was back with a vengeance.

Finn raised his hands. She needed to hear this.

"You're a person, Nat." She opened her mouth, but he pressed on before she could argue, "An amazing, beautiful soul who takes on far more than her share." Mentally, he sent a prayer to the universe that pushing her now wouldn't permanently drive her away. If it did, she still needed to hear it. "You took care of Uncle Warren by yourself for three years. You've been running yourself into the ground at Saddler's."

He took a step forward and opened his arms, hoping she'd let him take some of the burden she'd placed on herself.

"Do you have a point, Finn?" Natasha's eyes flashed, and then, the tears started again. "No. I am not crying. I am not."

The bravado drained from her as the tears fell and she dropped her head back into her arms. He whispered, "You cannot do it all, Nat. No one can. That doesn't mean you failed."

Natasha leaned back and rolled her eyes. The annoyed look didn't staunch the tears. His heart twisted as he looked at her. Deep circles highlighted her eyes, her skin was pale, and her cheek bones stood out—prominently. She looked like he looked when she'd read him the riot act three weeks ago.

"Have you been getting enough sleep?" He knew the answer but wanted to see if she'd own up to it.

Stepping out of his arms, she picked up her beer and slouched back into the chair. She tipped the bottle up, drained it, then sat it down. "I can't sleep for more than three hours before I wake up. Sometimes I can go back to sleep but usually I just have to push through."

Pure force of will was all that was keeping her moving, but she was at the wall. Straightening her back, she looked him in the eyes. "I am sorry for losing my control, again. It's not like me. I should probably get some coffee."

The last thing she needed was more caffeine, but she didn't give him time to point that out. She started to stand, but Finn grabbed her wrist. "You came looking for help. That's nothing to apologize for. You will always be welcome here."

She belonged here. When he'd thought of Nightfall while in California, Nat was in the kitchen, even though she hated cooking. Or she was on the oversize chair watching a movie. Nightfall and Nat were intertwined.

Not wanting to dwell on that thought for too long, he pushed forward. "Why do you only sleep three hours at a time?"

"It's not important, Finn. The computer needs fixed."

"I'll deal with the laptop in a minute," Finn interrupted before crouching next to her. He ran a hand over her tear-stained cheek, grateful when she didn't pull away. "Uncle Warren needed medications every three hours, didn't he?"

Natasha nodded, "My body got into the rhythm years ago. Can't seem to break it."

Standing up, he motioned for her to stay seated. Moving through the living room, Finn grabbed a box of tissues before heading back towards her. She gave a weak smile before blowing her nose in an unladylike snort. Natasha looked toward Warren's bedroom and smiled. For half a second, Finn almost expected his uncle to walk through the kitchen and greet him, but that fantasy was gone. As was whatever memory Natasha watched in the theater of her mind.

"There are times I think I might will him back," Finn offered.

"He'd have been so glad to see you." Her red-rimmed eyes floated with more tears, but they didn't fall. "He was so quiet when we were growing up. When reality struck, he opened up. We talked about so many things."

Thank goodness his uncle had her.

"He liked to joke that he only married me to keep me in trust for you." A giggle escaped her lips and her cheeks reddened, but she didn't take it back.

As she laid her head back down on the table, Finn traced the outline of her smooth face. The dusting of freckles across her nose lightened in the last decade, and her hair was no longer full of gold streaks from the sun. She was always taking care of others, but who was there to protect her?

Once, that was my job. Finn sighed at himself but smiled at her steadily. "Nat."

"I'm just so tired, Finnegan." The words were barely audible, but he suspected they cost her a lot to voice.

Exhaustion was a problem Finn knew how to fix.

"You need to rest. Take a nap upstairs while I figure this out." He motioned towards the computer. There was no way she'd sleep, if she thought he wasn't focusing on the damned laptop.

He wasn't surprised that her eyes shot open. She was going to argue, but he was not backing down. "Don't make me carry you. I will."

"That wouldn't be the worst thing." Her hand flew to her mouth, and she nearly knocked the chair over, pushing back to step away from him. "I'll go." She headed for the door, raising a hand as she raced from the room in embarrassment.

He'd have carried her. *Happily*

If that threat was what it took to get her to go take a nap, then that worked, too.

He was holding me in trust. Natasha's words reverberated through him. He couldn't think of that right now. He was going to fix her computer. If he had to pay the ransom, he would. Personally, he hoped there was a way to slay this dragon without giving it any gold.

Natasha rolled over, and Finn's scent invaded her senses. She took a deep breath, enjoying the soft, cinnamon coffee smell that always made her think of him. *Finn.*

She sat up as reality and the late sun crashed through the window. She'd told him she wouldn't mind if he carried her. Said the words out loud for everyone to hear.

No one there but us.

Her heart reminding her brain that no one else heard didn't drive the embarrassment from her. Sitting in this room wouldn't accomplish anything. She needed to see what was going on with her computer. Needed to know if she'd lost everything.

She hauled herself from the bed and headed down the stairs. Time to face the piper.

For the computer and my loose tongue.

Finn stepped around the corner as she hit the last step.

"Your files are fine." Finn knew she needed to know immediately. "I had one of my technicians go through your system. The hack wasn't as sophisticated as I feared. The virus hit your computer, not your cloud back up. The amount of data you lost should be only the last eight hours. My technician is still looking for those, too. Atticus is pretty amazing so, if anyone can find those files, he will."

"Now." He grabbed her hand and pulled her towards the kitchen.

Her laptop was not on the table, and she pursed her lips. She needed to get that and get out of his hair. She already took far too much of his day. She started towards the study, but Finn blocked her path.

"Nope. Sit." He pointed to a chair.

Bristling, she prepared for battle. She'd come for technical help and gotten a nap. Though, the computer issue was fixed, too. Everything was always better when Finn was around.

I missed that sense of security.

Still. She crossed her arms. "The computer?"

He put his finger against her lips. "You need to eat something, and we need to talk. I promise to return your laptop as soon as you have something to eat."

She almost planted her feet just to make a point as he directed her to the table, but the food smelled so good. Her mouth watered as he pushed a plate of lasagna in front of her.

"You cannot continue to be such a Mary Sue." Finn's eyes narrowed as he slid into the chair across from her and pointed to the lasagna.

She shook her head and grabbed the fork, but did not dip into the lasagna, even though the savory scent called to her stomach and soul. "Who the hell is Mary Sue?"

Finn chuckled, "God, I missed you."

Then don't leave. Those words stayed locked away. She gave into the growl of her stomach. Took a big bite of the lasagna, moaning as the sauce and noodles struck all the right taste buds.

Finn took a bite of his food, and then, he pointed his fork at her. "One of my favorite things about California is the San Diego Comic Con. In comics, and I think books in general, a Mary Sue character mirrors wish fulfillment. They are perfect at everything. They have no flaws. Think the original superheroes. Everything they do is right, for the right reasons."

"You think I do everything right?" For the last three years, she questioned every decision, every choice. Even those she'd had no option but to take. Perfect was not a descriptor she'd ever lay on herself.

"I think you are trying very hard to take care of everyone all the time. I think you want everyone to see you as perfect. You're damn close, honey, but perfection destroys. You have to take care of yourself."

"I'm not doing that much for people. Not anymore." She took another bite to avoid saying anything else.

Finn raised an eyebrow. "You cleaned my kitchen while I slept, Nat. After I was horrid to you."

"I was helping." She felt her lip tremble. "You were exhausted. You didn't even hear me come in."

Finn reached for her hand. Wrapping his fingers through hers. How many times had they sat at this table, just like this?

"*You* are exhausted, too. You have done nothing but take care of Uncle Warren and run Saddler's for your father for at least the last five years. I suspect you have been running Saddler's quietly for far longer."

"Mark told me about your master's degree. How did you get a graduate degree, run the store, and take care of Warren?"

"I had a dictation tool to help me. You weren't here to check my homework."

After everything she'd accomplished, why was she still so worried about grades? Why did it matter that she'd walked the stage without honors? She'd walked it. It stung that no matter how hard she worked, her grades had never matched her brothers.

"Nat, you are one of the smartest people I know. I was not talking about how you managed to pass classes. Hell, Nat, I hardly helped at all our last two years at The University of Wyoming. Your accomplishments were always yours. Stop downplaying yourself."

"When did you find time to study while taking care of Warren and the store?" His eyebrow quirked.

"I stayed up late most nights." She sighed and looked out the window. *Every night.*

No need to point out what he could guess. "Dad needed the help with everyone gone, and I was happy to give it. I love Saddler's."

"I know you do." There was a whisper of something in his voice. Something he cleared away as he stood.

"I guess I can return your property." He walked to the pantry and grabbed it from the top shelf. "You put my laptop in the pantry?"

"Figured it was the one place you wouldn't look, if you were angry enough to commence a search." He winked as he lifted it, but kept it held close to his body. "You were always allergic to cooking."

She stuck her tongue out. "You were always the better cook. Why bother with my burned entrees when I had a master?"

"I'll cook for you anytime you ask, Nat." Finn's soft gaze held hers.

Fire crackled between them. The spark was there, if she wanted to fan the flame.

Focus, Natasha.

She was here for tech support. Getting lasagna was a bonus. "The laptop, Finn."

"Nope, not yet. A few weeks ago, you told me I needed rest. An observation that was not incorrect, but honey, you are breaking."

Honey. The endearment hammered against her soul. Each time Finn used it, a tiny bit of the armor she'd thrown around her heart collapsed. She missed him.

What would happen if I stepped into his arms? If I put away the fear and focused on what I really wanted?

"You have been taking care of everyone for so long. You need to let someone take care of you, or at the very least, help you out. There is no shame in accepting help, Nat."

It was on the tip of her tongue to ask if he was looking to take over the job, but she restrained herself. "I'll consider it."

He took a deep breath. "You aren't the only one trying to learn that lesson. This was your home for three years. There are a lot of things up in the air still, but I would like your help to wrap up Warren's things. See, I'm learning, too."

"Which room do you want to start with? His documents are in the study." If they were focusing on that, then they weren't hovering dangerously close to talking about endearments and dinner. The unspoken words that were hovering in the air around them.

Finn chuckled. "I didn't mean today. *That* is the Mary Sue activity I'm talking about."

"Tomorrow?" She wanted to see him. Wanted to spend time with him.

Finn shook his head, "Can't. How about next week? I need to return to San Francisco for a few days."

"Sure," the word fell from her mouth as reality crashed against her. San Francisco. The life he created for himself while she was busy finding herself here. She wanted, needed, to leave before she begged to stay.

This wasn't her home anymore. It was Finn's. Once they cleared everything out, it would be someone else's. Life moved on. She started towards the front door. It was past time to go.

"I appreciate the advice, lasagna, and the IT support." His fingers wrapped around her wrist as she reached for the front door.

"Your computer?" He held out the laptop.

She let out a chuckle. Right, the thing that she came here for. "Thanks. Guess I'm still a little scatterbrained. Not used to napping."

"Anytime, Natasha."

His fingers were warm as they lingered on hers. The moment hung between them. The past wrapped around them as the future rushed forth. He was so close. An inch or so away. She could chase the dream and see, if this time, he'd choose her.

Instead of doing that, she offered a smile and pulled the door open. "Goodnight, Finn."

Chapter Nine

N‌at looked at her phone, then pushed it into her purse. Finn left for San Francisco days ago. He'd texted a few times. She'd responded each time. He was checking on Nightfall, the computer hack and her. Each one was a not-always-gentle reminder to take care of herself. She hadn't heard from him last night.

And I was too cowardly to make the first move.

Her watch buzzed. She needed to think of all that needed done at Saddler's, sitting in her truck overthinking wasn't accomplishing a thing.

She hopped out of the truck and headed to the front door. Pulling on the door, Natasha nearly bumped her head as it stayed in place. Locked. No, that wasn't right. Her dad was here.

The overhead lights buzzed above the rows of shelves. Clearly, he'd arrived. Frowning, she fished for her keys from her oversized purse. With any luck, her dad would realize he'd left the door locked before she dumped the bag's contents on the sidewalk.

"Should have cleaned this thing out weeks ago," she muttered as her fingers grazed what she hoped was a still wrapped granola bar. Finally, cool steel met her fingers. Hoisting her treasure from its hiding place, she cringed at the crumbs clinging to her fingernails.

Another thing to add to the ever-growing list of minor chores needing done.

Stepping into the store, she pulled the electric open sign. "Dad! You forgot to unlock the door." No salty reply echoed down the store. Silence. Nat started towards the back of the store, her feet picking up the pace with each step. "Dad!"

She opened the office door and everything froze.

"Hello? Hello? Herb." A faint cry called from the open line beside her father's limp hand, breaking the spell.

"Dad!" She was by his side in seconds that took forever. "Daddy?"

"Is someone there?" the voice on the other end of the line crackled.

"Daddy!" Her fingers shook as she laid them against his neck.

Please. Please. I can't lose him.

The bump under his skin seemed to echo throughout the room. He was still with her.

"I need someone to pick up the phone!" the voice called again.

"This is Natasha." Her words sounded hollow in the empty room. "Dad still has a pulse. He's breathing, but it's light."

"Natasha, it's Becky, from the firehouse. The paramedics are on their way, but I need you to answer some questions." The command echoed through the phone. Focus. This was an emergency and time mattered. She'd taken CPR classes. She knew what to do.

"You said he's still breathing; is he on the ground?"

"No, he's slumped over his desk." Natasha sucked in a breath as her mind pushed all the emotions back. There'd be time for that later. "His breathing is very shallow."

"Lower him to the ground and tip his head up. I need him in position in case we need to start CPR."

It was the right call. She knew that. Still, it didn't keep her heart from wanting to scream that it wasn't necessary. That everything was going to be fine.

Luckily, her mind was in control. His weight pressed against her as she lifted him. Dead weight was heavy, and she lost her grip as he slid to. She cradled his head, but her father's hip cracked against the floor. "I'm sorry."

He grunted. What a beautiful sound. Then his eyes open, gazing up at her unfocused but open. "Natasha?"

Her throat seized, but she pushed the words out. "Dad. Yeah. It's me."

"Natasha, what's going on?"

Lifting the phone, she brushed tears away. "He's awake, sort of. He recognized me, but he's groggy."

"I don't want to go to the hospital." He was going. Whether or not he wanted to.

"We're in Saddler's back office. You come straight through the store and turn right. The door is open." Nat explained to the operator, whose name she'd forgotten in the panic, exactly how to find the back office and hoped her father didn't plan to argue with the medical staff.

The operator offered a small chuckle. "I think everyone knows where the back office is, Natasha. The squad is there. You should hear them coming."

She looked up to see the first crew member walking through the door. "They're here."

"Alright. I am leaving you in their very competent hands." She clicked off without waiting for a response.

"Don't make a fuss," her dad attempted to wave away the first EMT.

She was grateful the young man told him he had no option but to take a trip with him, because Nat didn't know if she could manage it without screaming at him.

Dropping a light kiss against his cheek, Nat swallowed back her fears. "I'm right behind you, Dad. Love you," she whispered against his ear as they loaded him into the ambulance.

"I want to go home." The first time her dad complained, Natasha was grateful that his curmudgeonly nature was shining through. It had lost its appeal somewhere around hour two. And she had no patience in hour five.

"You had a heart attack. *Here* is where you need to be."

"Heart attack like event." Her father rolled his eyes, then glared at the monitors, keeping very close track of his vital signs.

She shifted in the uncomfortable chair. Patience. She needed patience. She was literally at the end of her rope with the complaints. "No splitting hairs. I found you slumped over your desk. So you are staying right there in that damn bed until the doctor says you are fine."

The door to the room swung open and Caleb, her oldest brother, slipped through. "Dad and Natasha arguing, if that doesn't sound like home, I don't know what does."

Standing, Natasha stretched before allowing Caleb to pull her into a tight hug. She patted his back as a small shudder went through him. "He's going to be alright. Although he should stop smoking and rest more."

"I am right here. No need to talk about me like I am not." He growled, then reached out a hand to Caleb. "You didn't have to come. They're going to let me go home any minute."

Her brother stepped to the bed and gripped her dad's hand. Caleb pushed a tear away, "It's not every day your dad has a heart attack like event. Figured I could spare a few hours."

"Why don't I take the night shift?" Caleb looked over his

shoulder at Nat, ignoring the ongoing complaints of *'I'm not staying.'*

Natasha grabbed her bag, far to happy for the reprieve. "Liam should be here tomorrow. He's on call at the vet hospital tonight, but he promised to be here by lunchtime."

Their father grunted as Natasha kissed his cheek. "No need for everyone to rush home. I'm fine. Overworked, and ready for retirement, but fine."

Ignoring the grumble, Natasha focused her attention on Caleb. "I need to run by the store. Pretty sure I left the door unlocked and the open sign on. Though, most of the town has spent at least a few minutes in the waiting room today."

Not Finn, though. She'd searched for him each time she'd exited the room, certain that now he'd be waiting. Mark had said he'd caught the red eye last night and arrived in Walkins this morning.

An answer to why he wasn't texting, but not for why he didn't stop by.

Why should he?

There was no reason for Finn to sit in an empty room doing nothing. No reason for him to seek her out. That didn't silence the ball of hope that he'd check in on her.

None of it mattered. Right now, she needed to lock up the store and fall into bed.

The drive from the hospital only took a few minutes. Parking the car, she was stunned to see Mr. Webber exiting the store, holding a bag. He waved before driving away. There was no way Mr. Webber was taking something. The man probably needed an item, or two, and simply left a note and a few bills next to the cash register.

"How's your dad?" The question hit her the moment she opened the door.

Natasha froze, staring at Finn, closing the register. The nightly restocking list was complete next to him, and she could tell he'd already cleaned the front.

Had he been here all day?

"Nat," he asked again. "Is he okay? Mark said they might release him tomorrow. Did something else happen?"

"He's going to be fine." They weren't the words she wanted to say, but they were the only ones that materialized.

Finn stepped from behind the register, moving toward her. "What are you doing here? You should be at the hospital?"

"What are *you* doing here?"

Finn thought it was fairly obvious what he was doing. She'd had a long day, and he wasn't going to push her buttons.

"Working," Finn motioned towards the full till. "I got back this morning." Raced back. Needing to see her. The few texts they'd exchanged had given him hope he didn't deserve. "I arrived as you pulled out of the parking lot behind the ambulance. The door was standing open."

The blood drained from Natasha's pale skin as she pinched the bridge of her nose. "Standing open?"

Finn tapped her nose lightly. "No beating yourself up, Nat. That is apparently your superpower, and I won't have it. You were focused on your dad. As you should have been."

Blowing out a sigh, Natasha looked around the store. "Thank you for the help, Finn. It was kind of you to stay all day, but I can see that everything is in order for the night."

"No." Two little forceful letters. He wanted to be clear. There was no way he was leaving. "You've had a long day. Let me help." He stepped around the counter and opened his arms.

She was in them immediately. Her shoulders relaxing. "He's going to be fine."

The words she couldn't utter echoed in the silence. She'd thought she might lose her father. She'd found him and spent all day taking care of everything at the hospital.

But Finn was here, now. Taking care of her.

Finn ran a hand along her back. Letting her soak in the comfort. "Today was a long day. So let's get this place closed up."

Nat sighed against his chest. "Fine, but you have to mop."

She let out a small giggle as she stepped back. Clearly shocked by the notes leaving her lips.

"I always hated that chore." Finn winked to lighten the embarrassment he saw blooming in her cheeks. She'd accepted his help and let him hug her. He was barely keeping the joyful shout rumbling through his chest in check.

"No shirking either," Natasha raised a finger, pointing it towards him as she repeated her father's common refrain.

He'd worked after school at Saddler's. Most of Walkin's population learned the proper way to mop a floor from Herb Saddler during their first or second jobs.

"I know we planned to meet up this weekend to go through things at the ranch, but with your dad, we can cancel. I'll get a feel for things and if I have questions, I can text you." He was looking forward to this weekend. To time together, even with a sad chore. He wasn't going to interfere if Herb was still ill. "Not too many texts. I promise. I just don't want to accidentally toss something that was important to Warren."

Or you.

She picked up her bag. "Honestly, I'd still like to come over. My brothers are in town. They can pitch in with Dad. I need to close off a few things in back. I'll be ready to close up as soon as the mopping is done."

He gave her a playful salute, enjoying the roll of her eyes as she headed to the office. The mopping had gone faster than he'd remembered as a teen. Before he knew it, he was standing next to her as she locked the door.

Natasha turned. The lone streetlight illuminated her freckles. "I could have done it all by myself, Finn."

"I know, Nat."

She hesitated for a moment before she leaned into him. "It was nice not to, though. Thank you."

The hug was over far too soon. It took all his self-control not to pull her back into his arms. He waited, hands tucked into his pockets, for her truck's engine to finally roll over before heading to his car.

***

Memories and dust hung in the air as Finn opened another box. Warren's life packed away into cardboard. Swallowing, he reached in and withdrew a few moth-eaten shirts that Warren had likely boxed up around the time Finn was in grade school.

Packrat, thy name was Warren.

"Not sure why he kept all this junk." Finn tossed each shirt, watching them land in the heap they'd designated as trash.

"I think he was worried about needing something later. Though how he thought he'd find it if he had to is beyond me." Nat giggled as she walked towards him with yet another box.

The stuff just kept coming.

"Enough about Warren's junk—and he called it that too— so I don't have to feel bad about it. Tell me about California." Natasha handed him another box marked papers and stuff, then headed back to the one she was going through.

"You don't want to talk about California, Nat." Finn didn't look up from the box marked Papers and Stuff. That was one way to describe the piles of papers appearing as his box knife cut through the tape. He'd always known Uncle Warren had little interest in paperwork, but how the man managed a ranch by just tossing papers into a box and putting the year, or not, on the side was a mystery. He doubted any useful documents were entombed in here, but they had to make sure.

Natasha didn't look up from the box where she was tossing more shirts into the heap. "These aren't even fit for rags. And sure, I want to talk about it. I'm curious about your life."

Finn gave her a small wink. "Uh, huh?"

"Finnegan, I was hurt when you left." Her jeweled gaze met his, "Saddler's is my dream." Nat's cheeks turned pink as she returned her focus to the box, "But I never rooted for you to fail. Your dreams didn't include Walkins, but you deserve to be happy wherever you plant your feet."

Natasha ducked behind another large stack of boxes, and the soft rustle of paper floated through the room. "I watch your yearly webcast. You on that great big stage. All the images flashing behind you. Better than the slide show Mark gave when he was going over farm contracts and state licenses for land use. He is so smart, but he could use your stage presence."

Warmth coated his body, and he was grateful she could not see the heat spreading up his neck. With each of his milestones, he always considered calling her. It was only the fear of her refusing his call, or that someone else might answer, that stayed his fingers.

"Warren loved watching them. He was really proud of you."

Those words cut through his thoughts. "He watched?"

"Of course. He told everyone in town and all the hospital staff about you. Everyone was suitably impressed, and I am pretty sure a few nurses had celebrity crushes on you."

He noticed she didn't offer to set him up with any of those nurses. Finn was grasping at every sign of hope.

"He was proud of me?" It wasn't until Natasha emerged from behind her roost that he realized he'd spoken the words.

"You were his greatest accomplishment." She slapped him lightly on the shoulder before withdrawing to her corner.

Finn always planned to return to Walkins a success. Show the investors he'd begged to fund his company that they'd made a mistake betting against him. No matter how much he achieved, though, it never seemed enough. None of the accomplishments he gained were shiny enough to cover all he'd lost. Friends, Warren, Nightfall.

Nat.

"Now I want cheerful talk. So, tell me about San Francisco." She clapped her hands, then put them on her hips as she issued the order.

What was there to say? He spent most of the time at the office. Eaten more take out that any person should and worked so hard he'd lost focus on everything else. "It's a lot different."

"Gee, don't be too descriptive Finn."

He laughed and shook his head. "I don't know how to describe it. It's a melting pot of humanity. I can order Thai food and have it delivered at 3 am. It's hilly and loud." He tried to picture the city, but his mind kept focusing on the open range of Warren's ranch. He'd traveled back and forth and lived there for ten years. Yet when he closed his eyes, nothing materialized.

"I thought the city was lovely, but I missed seeing the stars." Nat clucked her tongue, "Though I did like being close to the water. The bay makes the duck ponds here look like puddles."

His head spun at her casual tone. "When did you come to the city?"

She paused and poked her head around the corner. A line of dirt dashed across her cheek. Her lip puckered to the right, and she closed her eyes. Searching for the memory or for words to say? "Close to five years ago. It was just before you took your company public."

She'd been in his city. So close to him. And he'd never known. "You should have let me know. I could have shown you around." His words sounded stilted, and his chest hurt.

"You stood me up."

Depositing his stack of papers in the bin designated for shredding and recycling, Finn stepped into the small fort she'd created. Pushing a strand of red hair from her cheek, he let his finger linger for just a moment, grateful when she didn't pull away. "I would *never* stand you up, Natasha."

"Never?" Cocking her head to the side, she smiled, then shrugged. "I made the appointment with your secretary. I wanted," her voice trailed off.

She'd wanted what? Why was his Nat in San Francisco? The notation in his calendar must have been especially vague. Had he seen Nat's name, Finn would have cancelled every meeting to see what she wanted.

His heart clenched as his mind raced. Would he have cancelled everything or did he just want to believe that he could let something stand in front of Reach?

When Natasha started again, her voice was upbeat. To upbeat. "It was just a lunch date, Finn. Really, it's not a big deal. I had a good time walking around the city, sampling the food." She pursed her lips and let out a soft moan. "The food. Oh, what I wouldn't give for an Indian or Thai place in this town. None of the recipes I found online taste anything close to what I had there."

"That isn't too surprising." He needed to make the joke. Needed to focus on something else, even for just a moment. He'd never pictured her outside this town. On his darkest days, he'd grumbled that she should have at least tried it.

And she had.

"I made a few friends who I still keep in touch with. Social media is great for that. I spent my days bar hopping in some truly wonderful underground spots." She laughed. "It was a fun vacation. That was when I discovered how much I love to travel. That is one of Dad's excuses for not selling me all of Saddler's. He claims I won't travel anymore. Just because he doesn't."

She cleared her throat. Herb was doing better. So much better, but that was still a raw nerve. "I even got a tattoo!"

"A tattoo? No? You didn't." Nat in the big city had come home with a permanent reminder.

Laughing, she lifted the leg of her pants. A small heart-shaped locket with a broken key emblazoned across her ankle. He'd stood her up. Unknowingly, but still. And she'd gotten a permanent reminder.

"It suits you." Finn pulled his bottom lip through his teeth. "Never suspected that Natasha Saddler would wind up with a tattoo." The tease was half-hearted, but it was all he could manage after seeing it.

"Oh, that was just my first."

His eyes widen and mentally he started guessing where on her body he might find more ink.

Seeming to sense his interest, she playfully winked before changing the subject. "I need to get home; I have to be at the store early tomorrow. But I can come back tomorrow evening, after dinner, and help a bit more."

He nodded before hugging her tightly. Nat leaned into the hug. Their hearts seeming to sync. A ridiculous notion but holding her seemed to make everything right.

She smelled of sun, lemon, and dust. He placed a chaste kiss on her cheek, trying not to focus on the mystery tattoos. "Thank you for the help."

Unfortunately, he'd spend the rest of his days knowing the failed lunch date was permanently imprinted as a broken key on more than just her body.

Sweat poured down his back, and his feet burned as Finn finally turned back towards the house. Reach's sale was final without any grand fanfare. Documents signed and faxed. Money deposited in accounts. Life moved on.

He was staying in Walkins. The final meetings required his attention in San Francisco. He needed to gather his personal effects, sell his condo, figure out where to forward his mail. All that could be handled in a few days or weeks. Opening the door to his old room, he laughed at the small bed and assigned it as his project for the day. If he planned to stay, it was past time he moved into the master bedroom.

The closet door creaked as he pulled it open and for a minute, he looked over his shoulder, waiting for Warren's yell.

Groping along the top shelf, Finn hauled down an old record. He smiled at the well-worn cover as memories pushed away the wave of grief the creak caused. Uncle Warren hated the mp3s that dominated during Finn's high school time.

Though aren't records back in vogue now?

Chuckling, he ran a finger along the cover before dragging the rest out of the closet. Happy memories floated down with dust. Finn jumping around the living room, dancing as the records skipped. This home held so many wonderful memories of mismatched rhythms as he carried his treasure to the bed. A large manila envelope slipped from between two vinyl's and thumped to the floor. In his handwriting, it declared, '*Only to be opened by Finn,*' on the front to match the scrawl of, "*I mean it Natasha, if you find this, put it down,*' on the back.

Laughing, Finn took the package to the bed and shook it carefully. Things shifted inside, but the contents made no noise.

What could my uncle have wanted me to see?

It was just like his uncle to stick it between old records. "It's a good thing I found it."

He looked out the window at the horse barn. Finn didn't really believe in ghosts, but if Warren could pick his paradise, he'd be out there. Riding and caring for horses.

Finn turned back to his prize. His finger hovered for several moments as he tried to convince himself to slit the top. A message from the grave could not be unread. Closing his eyes, he slid a finger under the flap and dumped the contents.

A packet of pictures fell into his lap. Finn's head jerked back. He wasn't sure what he'd expected, but it wasn't this. The first image was his parents standing at the altar, then his mother holding him in the hospital, and love highlighted through bright Kodak tones. Finn's memories of his parents were hazy. More like feelings of love and safety than genuine memories. They looked so young and happy.

An image of Finn and Warren standing next to each other while facing the back of the ranch followed. It was a standard cowboy photo. Warren in the prime of his life, and Finn's body was undergoing the shift from boy to man. It must have been taken some time in the year before he'd surpassed his uncle's height.

Methodically working his way through his childhood, Finn sent a silent thank you that Warren bothered to maintain a record. His boxes were a disorganized mess, but this was all in order. Laughter echoed in the room as Finn relived memories, he long thought he had assigned to the waste bin of history. School dances, bad haircuts, and science competitions culminated in the final image.

Natasha stood next to him while holding up her hand and proudly displaying the tiny diamond ring.

A knot formed in his throat, and he laid that memory apart from the others. Lifting the folder, he reached in, hoping for a few more happy snapshots. Instead, two small envelopes reached him. A simple one and two labeled each respectively.

Leaving the bed scattered with photos, Finn headed for the kitchen. Laying the letters on the kitchen table, he grabbed a beer and leaned against the counter. Answers lay in two, tiny pieces of paper, so discarding them wasn't an option. Pulling deeply on the beer, Finn marched towards them and opened number one.

Scratches of Warren's writing met Finn's gaze, and he lifted the paper, wishing the aroma of leather and horse met his nose rather than paper. In his memory, Uncle Warren's handwriting was strong, if not pretty, but the words that greeted him seemed written with considerable effort.

Finn,

If you are reading this, I've passed into the next phase of existence. I want you to know three things.

One, I love you and am so proud of you. You are my greatest success, and I know my sister and your father are smiling down at the man you've become. No doubt, if I am fortunate enough to meet them in the next realm, your mother is peppering me for stories about you.

Two, I am sorry I never told you about Natasha. I was scared after my diagnosis, and by the time I thought through the consequences of our marriage, she was my wife. She is an amazing woman and was my rock during the difficult years of doctor's appointments and failed treatments. I should have told you. Something she has stated repeatedly. The blame lies with me, not her.

Three, Natasha would kill me if she knew I was writing this final line—terminal humor joke—funny, I promise. She still loves you. You love her, too. I hear it every time you ask about her. I have always believed you were soulmates, if such a wonderful thing exists. She's waiting for you, but she will not wait forever, nor should she. She deserves a partner who puts her first and loves her more than anything. You are capable of this. If you can't be that man, walk away from Walkins and never come back. The second envelope contains the letter she wrote after you left. If you have no intention of pursuing her, burn it without opening.

I will always love you.

Until we meet again,

Uncle Warren

Knocking the empty beer can against the kitchen table, Finn tried to find the courage to open the final letter. He'd never stopped loving Natasha.

What if she doesn't want me anymore? What if she does?

Throwing his fears aside, he picked up the letter. If he didn't try, he'd die wondering what might have been. Cracking the second seal, he braced himself. The small letter unfolded, and he stared at its simple words.

Finnegan,

Chasing dreams is important. I will be here whenever your dreams turn you back to home.

All my love,

Nat

Reaching for the wall, Natasha tried to breathe as she focused on her position. Normally, yoga calmed her nerves or at least quieted her mind. Today the rambling thoughts kept tumbling around. Stepping into downward dog, she paid attention to the lengthening of her calf and noticed the paint on her toenails was chipping. Perhaps she should paint them a bright purple.

"Get it together," she muttered. She took a deep breath, forcing her thoughts away from pretty nail polish and actively trying to clear her head. It might have worked, had her stomach not added its thoughts to the day. Finally, she gave in and allowed her mind to follow the meandering paths that might lead to a snack, while she lifted her right leg and focused on the wall. Salty or sweet became her new mantra, and her stomach clambered for both.

A knock at the front door was an answer to a prayer. At least she had a good reason for not paying attention. Perhaps she'd try another hour tonight before bed.

"Finn." Natasha smiled as she pushed a loose strand of hair behind her ear, trying to remember the last time she opened the door to someone other than her ex-fiancé. He looked relaxed and comfortable as he leaned against the door frame.

"Hi." How did a man manage to look so sexy in rumpled blue jeans and faded t-shirts?

She stepped back and waited for him to come in.

The duplex's rent was cheap, but it didn't give her much room for entertaining. Rolling up her mat, she kept her back to Finn before realizing he enjoyed a full view of her ass in the very tight yoga pants. Standing up, she hoped her cheeks weren't flaming, but the heat in her face meant she probably looked like a tomato.

Finn's face was blank, though his eyes glittered. "Am I interrupting?"

"Yes, you are." Placing her hands on her hips, she tried to

look imposing but couldn't hold the serious face. Interruption was what Finn had always done best. Interrupting her studies, interrupting her plans, interrupting her happy ending, and now, he was interrupting her attempts to never think of him again. And she yearned for each interruption.

She shot him a playful glare. "The distraction is a welcome one. Though. I wasn't exactly focused. So good time for you to stop by. What brings you to my door? More boxes to sort through or documents to sign?"

His eyes shifted, and a frown crossed his lips before being replaced by a slightly-off smile. "Just came to see if you wanted to go get some ice cream. Or maybe a burger and then some ice cream."

A polite refusal was on the tip of her tongue, but she couldn't force the words out. She wanted to spend time with him. Her heart only felt complete when she was with Finn. A few weeks of happiness were better than a lifetime of emptiness.

So instead of saying it was nice he invited her, but no thank you, she nodded. "Just let me change." She set the water down and dashed up the stairs, not sure what she might say if she stayed longer. In her haste, she accidentally slammed her bedroom door. Her eyes wide, she stared at the offending wood as the echo reverberated down the staircase.

"Good grief, Natasha!" She hugged herself before grabbing a soft pair of blue jeans and a pink blouse. "You can do this. It's just dinner."

There was no way to pretend the pep talk worked. Just dinner with a man her heart had never recovered from. She wasn't sure how this ended but she didn't care. She knew he'd leave. No illusions this time. So why not focus on having a good time for a little while?

The Greasy Spoon was the only unaltered place in Walkins. Its thick red leather booths were still pot marked with grease dribbles. The counter was the same, ugly, lime green it had been since before he was born. Even the menus, though they'd been reprinted, were the same. Only the prices were adjusted to account for inflation, but not by a significant amount.

Most of the booths were full, the tables covered by malt shakes, burgers and fries. The hum of small talk and kids laughing mixed with the odor of salt and grease. If Finn traveled back thirty years, the only difference would be people's outfits. The Greasy Spoon was the closest thing to a Welcome Center the town of Walkins had, and it was magnificent.

For the last hour, they'd relived the glory days of high school and college. Though, Natasha avoided any stories involving just the two of them. The years they'd spent engaged were also blessedly kept from the discussion. She'd laughed and joked, but her eyes kept darting to the other customers.

"Ashamed to be seen with me?" Finn kept his tone light, but the hint of fear was clear. He wanted her to have fun. She seemed to be, except that she avoided looking at anyone who passed their booth. People had looked. If she'd made eye contact, they'd have stopped for a chat.

Which people were clearly hoping for. No private dinner out in Walkins.

Picking up a limp fry, Natasha stared at it, not meeting his gaze. "No. Just wondering how many calls my father has received in the last hour, and how many text messages people left on my cell since the last time I checked."

"How many were there?"

"Fifteen texts and two missed calls," she gave him a crooked smile.

"And now?" A pit formed in the small of his belly. He'd wanted to spend time with her, needed her company. He hadn't counted on small town gossip caring about two, grown adults having a pleasant conversation in a dive burger joint.

Except everyone brought their dates to The Greasy Spoon. That knowledge hit him square in the face. Nothing went unnoticed here, and everything had a secret meaning to the locals. She shrugged, "It's not important, Finnegan. Sorry, Finn."

"You can call me Finnegan anytime you want." He'd been Finn to everyone for years. He hadn't lied when he told her it was more professional. At least, that was what his first angel investor had said. Finn had taken his three million dollars and the name suggestion.

But he wanted to hear his name roll from her lips freely. *And often.* Clearing his throat, he asked, "How many missed calls are there, Nat?"

"Only five" She slid the phone across the table and gave a sheepish smile. "And thirty-some texts. The Greasy Spoon and gossip. If that isn't a Walkin's Welcome Home, I don't know what is. People just taking guesses on whether it's a date."

Her skin was warm and soft. Her fingernails a subtle blush color, though he noticed a few cracks starting to show.

"What if this is a date?" The question was out before he thought about it. "What will the gossips say then?

Color traveled across her face before she pulled her hand away and placed her phone back in her purse. Nat dipped another fry in ketchup. "The talk isn't malicious, generally. People like to talk and eventually topics revert to the people you know."

No answer to the first question.

"In Walkins, most people know most everyone, so the same stories get passed around. When Mark dyed his hair blond, the discussion lasted almost a month passed when he dyed it back. When I got my first tattoo, the conversation floated around town for six months."

Where were those works of art hiding on her body? It took Finn a few seconds to realize what she'd said before it. "Mark dyed his hair blond? I may have to give him a hard time."

Natasha grimaced and shook her head. "I wouldn't. He did it to please Tabitha; she thought some movie star with the color was hot. He dyed it back the day after she left town. Not the best memory to bring up."

Finn nodded and then refocused, "How many tattoos do you have?"

She laughed and winked. "Nobody knows but me. I have more than one and less than twenty."

"Is that the answer you give everyone?"

A giggle filled the booth, and she covered her mouth with her hand. "Actually, the only people who have ever asked are the men who wanted to see me naked and you."

Finn's stomach clenched at the joke. He wanted to see all those tattoos, run his fingers down her hips and make her pupils dilate with pleasure. Nat in his arms, one with him. Finn licked his lips as he tried to stop the grip of need.

She grabbed a menu and frowned. "You promised me ice cream, are we ordering here, or do we set the tongues really wagging and head down to Maggie's?"

"There is a huge part of me that wants to see if we can get you to ten missed calls. So, I vote for Maggie's. Plus, I really want a scoop of her peanut butter chocolate chip on a brownie."

Tonight felt like old times. They had been as they once were, just Nat and her Finnegan. He wasn't ready for the spell to break.

Natasha slid her arm through Finn's as they exited Maggie's Dairy Bar. Her step caught, but Finn didn't pull away. It seemed natural, and she wanted to pretend for a few minutes more.

"Want to walk in the park?" Natasha's belly was full, but she wanted more time, as much as she could get with Finnegan.

Finn patted her hand. "That sounds like an amazing plan. Think I can still climb to the top of the wooden play set?"

Natasha laughed, "No, but only because they tore it down about six years ago. It didn't meet the new state safety standards." She, Mark, Scarlett, and most of their graduating class had gathered to watch the old castle structure come apart. It had played host to their childhood imaginations and been the location of more than one make-out session for almost three generations of Walkins' residents.

Finn whistled, "That's a shame. How will the youngsters learn to pull out splinters? Where will the teenagers learn to kiss?"

Nat hit her hip against his. "The youngsters' playground is so safe. I doubt they will need to learn how to pull a splinter until they are old enough to watch a how-to video online."

Clicking his teeth, Finn wrapped his arm around her shoulder. It was a safe gesture and so unsatisfying. "And the teens?"

Heat creeped up Nat's cheeks as she stared at the horizon. "I think today's teens are just as ingenious as we were to find places to be alone."

"I suppose so," Finn rested his head against hers.

What are we doing? Nat's chest clenched as she absorbed Finn's heat. Were they on a date? He'd asked. She hadn't answered for fear of being wrong. It felt like it. Maybe she just wanted it to be.

Biting her lip, she stepped away from him. Finn's face was

still as she walked towards the giant log puzzle the town council had added to the park a few months ago. If she didn't keep her hands busy, Nat was going to run them through Finn's hair and beg him to kiss her.

"Bet I can beat you." Natasha smiled as Finn raised an eyebrow.

Bending, he helped her stack the pieces. "Willing to place a real bet on that, Nat?"

"Sure." The word left her lips before she had time to think about it. Bets with Finn were always a little dangerous.

"If I win, you answer any question I ask. If you win, I will answer anything you want."

Dangerous indeed. "A question?" Natasha studied him. What did he want to know? Only one way to find out. "Get ready to spill all your secrets."

The tower toppled to the ground ten minutes later, and Natasha cheered. "Take that, Finnegan."

He laughed and started rebuilding the tower. "I demand a rematch."

"Fine, but I still get to ask a question." What did she want to know? So many questions floated in her mind as he rebuilt the tower. Did he miss her as much as she missed him? Did he wish they were playing out here with their children? Did Finn wish they could turn back time? Her tongue stuck to the roof of her mouth. Swallowing, Nat put the last piece on the stack. "What are you going to do now that Reach is gone?"

"I'm not completely sure." He stared at the setting sun and shrugged. "I have an idea, but it's in its infancy, and I don't know if it's even possible yet."

Is that company in California too? She'd already run through her supply of courage, so that question stayed buried. "I saw your former CFO is taking a position at another startup."

She'd followed the news about Reach for years. When the news hit her inbox this morning that a high-ranking member of the board had accepted a position at an artificial intelligence company, Natasha expected it to be Finn. She'd been so excited to discover it was someone else. *Too excited.*

"Yes, Michael was very excited about Stix's offer. He wanted me to join the board too but I declined."

Natasha's hand slipped, and the tower tumbled. Finn turned the offer down. Did that mean he wanted to stay? Or was he waiting for a better offer?

"My turn." Finn winked.

A deal was a deal. Natasha met his gaze; her heartbeat was pounding in her ears as Finn stepped up to her. The world disappeared as he looked at her. What did he want to know?

"What would you do if I kissed you?" Finn's fingers burned as they traced her jaw.

"Only one way to find out."

They'd kissed thousands of times, but this kiss, this soft exploratory embrace, was new. Finn's lips brushed hers, demanding nothing and everything. Home. That was who Finn was. It didn't matter how long they'd been apart, or the different paths they'd traveled. He was her Finnegan, the holder of her heart.

He pulled back and smiled. "Nat."

"I should get home." It was a cowardly response. She hated it, but her feet moved towards the center of town. If she didn't leave, she was going to beg him to stay forever. He had a plan. One in its infancy, but a plan. A goal.

His steps matched hers. "I had fun tonight."

"Me too, Finn."

Cows happily munched grass and basked in the afternoon sun as Finn pulled up to the small building where Mark kept his part-time law office. Examining the little building, Finn grinned. Mark's name plate stood out on the front door of a tiny home.

The crisp smell of paper and ink greeted him as Mark sat behind the desk while typing on a keyboard and talking on a headset. Motioning for Finn to take a seat, Mark returned to his phone conversation, quickly ending it. "Sorry, I expected that call to end thirty minutes ago."

Shaking his head, Finn gestured towards the office. "This is impressive."

Looking at his private space with pride, Mark nodded. "A few years ago, Micah Anderson made this his combined senior math and shop project."

Whistling, Finn ran his hand across a smooth board. "Hope he got an A."

Laughter filled the office as Mark sat back in his chair. "Yeah, made the bookshelves his peers created look pretty dismal. The young man has his own construction business. His last tiny home was featured on television and netted him a huge profit. Kid's going places."

Gesturing for Finn to take his seat, Mark returned to business. "You are not paying me by the hour to tell you about my home office." He typed on the computer then turned the laptop towards Finn showing a huge list of documents.

"I didn't realize I had such an extensive file with you," Finn joked.

Mark tilted his head, "I assumed you were here to discuss Nightfall Ranch when you called to schedule this appointment. Is there a different legal issue you wish to hire me for?"

"No, I'm here to discuss Nightfall." Pulling a small tablet from his backpack, Finn tried to focus. "I need to know what I can do with the property. What restrictions are there?"

"As I told you earlier, your uncle's will stipulates—"

"No, I'm not here to request you look for loopholes in the document you drew up. If I wanted that I'd hire another firm."

Mark crossed his arms. "I know that wasn't a dig, but I guarantee that document is solid. Hire any expensive firm you wish to try it."

"Sorry, I didn't mean any harm. It's just that Natasha mentioned state licenses, and I know right now it's zoned for farming, but what if it wasn't?"

"You're not planning on selling it?" Mark sat back in his chair, a smile on his lips.

"I'm not." Finn let out a sigh. It was so nice to say it out loud. He hadn't been a hundred percent certain of his choice until last night. Until Nat's lips met his. Their encounter had been too brief, but if it took the rest of his life, Finn was going to win her back.

Mark grinned. "I feel honor-bound to tell you that if you wanted to sell, there are several buyers who would be interested in the property. The land alone is worth almost two million."

Shrugging, Finn stated, "I don't exactly need money."

Mark leaned forward, resting his hands on the palm of his hands, "I heard Reach just sold for a tidy profit. I didn't know you were looking to get rid of it."

Not wanting to discuss the company's sale, Finn uttered, "Wasn't my idea, but that is a discussion that is going to require you to be off duty and a couple of beers."

"Fair enough, but what do you want to do with Nightfall?"

Swallowing his apprehension, Finn spun the tablet, letting Mark see the rudimentary mock-up of his idea. "I was thinking of building a technology school with a focus on agriculture. I can maintain some of the farmland, so the students can track their technology and apps in a real-world situation. I can bring horses back. I love the beasts and there is monitoring that can be improved for maintaining livestock."

"Wow."

"I'm not trying to change Walkins," Finn continued. "Well,

not too much. Agriculture takes so much work, which surprises no one. I know there are apps, but most are developed by people who don't actually farm. This way, the people that use it are at the forefront of development. What do you think?"

"Are you asking my permission?" Mark lifted his head from Finn's project notes.

"No. Maybe?"

"I think it's a good idea, but I am a lawyer, not a tech guru. So why ask me?"

Nat is the one you should ask. He needed to tell her, but he wanted to surprise her. Wanted her to see that he meant it when he said he was staying. Show her the proof.

"The land needs rezoned?" It was a weak excuse.

Mark chuckled, "You know how to rezone property Finn. Why are you really here?"

Finn took a deep breath. He needed to repair more than his relationship with Nat. "I missed you. I miss our easy friendship." Before Mark could respond, Finn continued, "I also miss Walkins. I spent so much of my youth plotting my exit, but this is home."

Pulling a hand through his hair, Finn continued, "Reach failed here. I couldn't get any buy in, let alone investors. I'm older, wiser and capable of kicking this off on my own." Finn hesitated, "Still, I don't know if my ideas will be welcome here. You know the town."

"If your ideas are welcome or you?" Mark raised an eyebrow.

Swallowing the lump in his throat, Finn shrugged, "Both."

He spent his childhood listening to people compare him to his parents. They'd run their teachers, their parents, and everyone else crazy. When they'd died base jumping after his third birthday, the town had been sympathetic, but no one acted surprised. No matter what Finn did, he always seemed to be compared to the sometimes-irresponsible parents he barely remembered.

"This is a great idea. One Walkins will welcome." Standing, Mark reached his hand out. "Welcome home, Finn. I admit I'm surprised you're still here, but I'm glad. I missed you, too."

Letting out a breath, Finn shook his old friend's hand. "Thanks. I'm more than a little surprised, too. I stayed away when I first left because I thought that if I came home, I'd never leave. Guess I wasn't wrong."

"And the woman you left behind?" Mark stared at Finn as he gulped his water. "I heard more than once about last night."

"I still love her. She's not keeping me at arm's length anymore. We had burgers and ice cream. It went well." Finn wasn't discussing their kiss. It was too fresh, too new. That was a moment for them alone.

"I know," Mark laughed. "My mother wanted all the details about your trip to The Greasy Spoon."

"Nothing goes unnoticed in Walkins. Not sure it really counted as a date." That wasn't true either, but until he knew Nat wanted more than a soft kiss in the park, Finn wasn't going to spread any gossip.

"Not really a date?" Mark lifted an eyebrow before adding, "I heard you left Maggie's together holding hands?"

"She had her arm through mine, but we weren't holding hands. You shouldn't listen to all the gossip." Last night had been one of the happiest of his life. His heart almost felt full again

"Nat's never stopped caring for you. I suspect it won't take long for her to fully trust you. She's too trusting as it is." Mark closed his computer, motioning for Finn to follow him to the door. Mark grabbed his shoulder as Finn stepped towards his car, "Listen, tonight's bowling night, so you should come."

"I'm there." He'd missed to many nights with friends.

"Tuesday is our standing night. It'll be nice to have another guy on the team." Mark let out a playful shudder, "Fair warning, the women are savage."

The bowling alley was loud! In the best way. Happy conversations, loud cheers, and a few boos directed at the pins, echoed over him, as he made his way down the busy lanes. It seemed most of his old buddies still made it to league night.

"You came." Mark slapped Finn's shoulders.

"I haven't been in a bowling alley in a long time." Finn smiled, as they headed towards lane five.

"Good." Mark chuckled as he walked towards their lane. "Natasha and Lauren beat me every week. It will be nice not to be last for once."

Lauren patted Mark lightly on the shoulder before shrugging. "It's hardly our fault your game is so terrible."

"Or that you blow in from out of nowhere and average two-fifty," Mark teased.

Natasha turned halfway in the plastic chair and smiled at him. Her bright yellow shorts shifted, and a hint of ink glinted on her thigh. What might be there? "I already added you."

Her words broke his mental wanderings on the ink, and Finn glanced at the screen. Geekman was listed below Lawman and Teach. Natasha's tagline was listed first, Farmgirl.

"No shirts?" Finn joked as he slid next to Mark. An ocean of rainbow polyester covered each lane. The other lanes looked darn close to professional.

"Our schedules haven't been regular enough in the last few years to make the commitment to a team. We come when we can, just to show up the rest of these guys." Mark laughed as he shook hands with someone in the other lane.

"Good to see you, Mark." Brad shook Mark's hand before turning his gaze to Finn. "And you too, stranger."

Finn barely kept his anger in check as Brad reached his hand across the plastic chairs as though he hadn't threatened Nat a few weeks ago. "How are things?"

The man ignored the less-than-friendly pressure Finn added to his grip. "Can't complain. Business is brisk, life stays busy. How are you doing, Natasha?"

Finn's insides tightened at Brad's simple question. He certainly didn't seem concerned about fraud tonight. Finn hadn't found a way to discreetly ask if Brad's company had paid Natasha's settlement, but Finn suspected she'd have mentioned the sizeable sum if Brad had. The salesman's eyes slid towards' Finn before smiling at Natasha.

"Their one date was disastrous," Mark whispered over the falling pins.

"I'm not surprised, the man seems more focused on himself than anyone else." Though it wasn't competition from Brad that he was worried about. Finn kept his eyes trained down the lane as he tested the weight of his bowling ball.

"Wasn't aware you knew Brad?" Mark pulled the ball out of Finn's hands, replacing it with another. Its weight spread more easily through his palms, but the thumb hole bit into him, so he passed it back and chose another.

"I ran into him a few weeks ago at Winen's. He was chatty." Finn was glad when Mark let the exchange go.

Natasha gestured towards the board, "Are we going to kick the boys' butts?"

"Oh, they are going down!" Lauren jumped to her feet, blowing a stray bang from her eyes as she shook Nat's shoulders, prepping her for the first throw.

"Little blood thirsty, this one," Finn hooked a finger towards Lauren as he looked at Mark.

"She's amazing." Mark coughed, then added, "At bowling. Her game is amazing."

Finn wondered if Lauren knew how much her friend wanted to be more. Since Finn was still in love with the woman preparing to pitch her ball down the lane, he elected not to tease Mark.

"Strike," Natasha cheered and twirled as she headed back towards the seats. "Beat that, Geekman!"

The lights faded as Natasha's last pin fell to the side. She turned, taking a bow, "I do think that spare cements my win."

Finn rolled his eyes, but he offered her a brilliant smile. "Two-twenty-six to ninety-eight. You *really* needed that spare. We closed the bowling alley."

Natasha turned as the emptiness and silence finally registered. "What time is it?" Finn raised his phone to show her the clock. Midnight was just around the corner, "Guess it's a good thing I have tomorrow off."

"You don't have to go home, but you can't stay here," Cindy said as she walked over with a broom.

"How much do I owe you?" She'd only paid for three games.

Cindy smiled and shook her head. "I haven't seen you truly let loose and have fun in years. The rest of your games are on the house." Then she turned to Finn, "You owe fifty-one."

"Best money I've spent in years." Finn winked and then motioned to the door. "Come on, I'll walk you out."

"Thanks for staying to play with me." She swallowed, trying to work up the courage to kiss him. It was all she'd been able to think about today. Last night's kiss had been wonderful, and she'd tossed and turned castigating herself for walking away.

Nat wanted to step into Finn's arms, pull his head towards her and see where the night took them. Instead, she slid her key into the door of her truck. *Coward!*

"Anytime Nat." Finn leaned against her truck, opening her door. "I'm staying until I know this ancient thing is going to start."

"No knocking the truck." Rolling down her window, she placed a chaste kiss on his cheek. "Tonight was a blast. Thanks again."

Finn tapped her nose and then motioned for her to start the engine. With a dramatic motion, Natasha turned the key. Unfortunately, the engine only coughed. She cursed and then stamped her foot against the gas while turning the key yet again. The engine refused to make any noise, and Finn seemed to be trying hard not to lose control.

"You cursed my truck!" She wagged a finger at him. Her truck was almost forty and on its second engine. This was becoming a more frequent problem. She should use some of her savings to purchase a reliable used one, but this vehicle was more than just transportation. *Memories don't get you to work, though.*

Finn opened the passenger's side door and slid in. "I remember sitting in this truck when the bed still had paint."

Patting the steering wheel, she smiled before scooting closer to him. "I learned to drive in this piece of junk and made out with a boy for the first time in it, too."

He squeezed her shoulder. "That was a good night."

"Who said it was with you?" She laughed as he made a playful sour face.

"This keeps happening, though. Shoot, it was twenty-plus years old when I bought it. It needs a new engine, again, and some new wiring. Not worth the price when I can get something in better shape for less money."

Finn put his arm around her shoulder, kissing her forehead as she leaned her head against him. "Remember how we used to drive up to the lake to fish?"

"Did we fish?" Her cheeks flamed at her flirty tone. At least there was no way for him to see the heat in her cheeks in the dark parking lot.

His low chuckle sent small, electric shocks straight to her toes. People weren't supposed to keep ancient trucks or refuse to move on from their high school sweetheart. But here she was, hoping he'd kiss her. Really kiss her.

Her heart would break when he left Walkins. Chased whatever dream he was cooking up. But she'd put herself back together once and could do it again. Tonight, she was getting what she really wanted.

"Take me home?"

"Of course." He slid a finger down her jaw and pressed his lips to her cheek. "Let's go."

The trip to Nat's took less than ten minutes, Finn wanted to scream as each red light turned green before he could even hit the break. Didn't the universe know he needed all the time possible with her?

"Finn." Natasha smiled, but she made no move to exit his car as he pulled to a stop in front of her home. She laced her fingers through his.

His thumb stroked the inside of her wrist as his fingers ached to do so much more.

Finn bent his head, the world disappearing as her lips met his. Berries, sunshine and perfection. That was the only descriptor for her kisses.

Nat's fingers ran through his hair as her mouth opened to his exploration. There was no other woman for him. She was the missing piece of his soul, and he'd stayed away far too long.

Sitting back, he rubbed his thumb across her cheek. Grey eyes dripping with desire stared at him. "Sweetheart, if you want to spend the evening alone, you need to step out of this car."

A finger slowly traced along his groin, and Finn slipped a hand up her shirt. Her skin was fire beneath his fingers. Her breath hitched. Running a finger along the outline of a nipple through her bra, Finn bent his head, dropping feathery kisses against the base of her neck.

"You are in charge here, Nat. Whatever you want."

"I think you should come in," she breathed.

Reaching for the door, Finn smiled as her jerky movements mirrored his. Cool evening air greeted them as he followed her to the duplex's front door. Distance was impossible to keep, even if he wanted too. His lips pressed to the back of her neck as his hand slid up her belly.

"I missed the feel of your skin," he groaned as he slid his hand to the base of her bra. He chuckled as she let out a breath.

"Finn, I need to get this door open before Mrs. Yeager comes to check on me. I would prefer not to explain to my eighty-year-old landlady why your hand is so far up my shirt."

Wrestling the key from her hand, Finn quickly unlocked the door and pulled her through. Closing the door, he pressed her against the wall. The urge to carry her upstairs and bury himself in her was overwhelming. Fighting the red flame of lust, he slipped her shirt over her head.

Nat. His Nat. Here. Now.

"Finn," Natasha rasped, placing her hands under his shirt with her fingernails gently scraping down his abs. "We have all night for you to make love to me."

"I know, sweetheart," he needed to slow down. The years since he'd been with her faded away as he remembered the subtle ways she loved to be touched. She lifted his shirt over his head, and he focused all his attention on her breasts in the sexiest, black, lace bra.

Arching against him, her fingernails dug sharply into his back. Pulling her shorts down, she slipped a hand between them and slid the zipper of his pants lower. Hungry demanding fingers stroked him, forcing his jeans to his knees. Finally, she begged, "Go slow later, right now, I just need you inside me. Please!"

The plea broke the minuscule amount of control he had left. He lifted her, bracing her against the wall. Shifting the thong to one side, he buried himself to the hilt.

Grabbing her ass, he pounded her against the door. This wasn't the way he'd planned to make love to her again. But they were both caught in the moment. Focused completely on this first reunion.

"Finn," Natasha's scream echoed through her small apartment as he drove into her.

"Nat. My Natasha," he cried as her groans grew louder. Leaning her head against his shoulder, he smiled as she gave into pleasure. As her climax flowed through him, he felt his own release build and willingly gave into it.

Tracing a finger down her throat, Finn tried to gain some control as he stared at Nat, slowly lowering her to the floor. He didn't like even the small amount of distance between them.

He lifted her back into his arms, this time cradling her. "I seem to remember you wanting me to carry you."

"I don't think that was quite what I said, but I am not complaining." Savoring her sweet warmth, he briefly glanced at their discarded pants and decided to grab those in the morning.

Fluttering kisses pressed against his neck and chest, as he gently placed Natasha on the bed before pulling away.

"Finn."

"I intend to make love to you again, honey but," he

flipped the switch and smiled, as she blinked at the light. "I need the light to find the rest of those tattoos."

A small honeybee was hovering above its hive on her left thigh. Delicate wings fluttered around the bee, giving it the appearance of flight. His fingers traced the outside of her thigh as he ran his other hand over her stomach.

"You taste like honey, so this one makes sense."

Laughing, she pulled him towards her. "I also used to keep bees, so it is more a remembrance of a very brief hobby."

Resisting her embrace nearly broke him, but Finn dropped a light kiss on her lips before pulling back. "I always assumed the first time I made love to you again would be slow and gentle. I plan to live that fantasy."

"You've thought of this?" A slight blush covered her body as Nat reached for him, again.

"A few times a week since I left. Every, single day since I returned. It's always been you, Nat. Always."

Dipping his head, he caught whatever she planned to say between his lips. Warmth spread through him as her body molded against his. Clasping at the hooks of her bra, his fingers fumbled.

Languidly smiling, Natasha leaned back and winked at him. "Forgotten how to unhook a bra, Finnegan?"

She deftly unhooked the lacy contraption before dropping the dainty piece of clothing off the bed. Focusing on the release of her breasts, Finn let his hands roam across the base of her breasts, enjoying the sighs of pleasure she released. Stroking a nipple, he watched it rise and then smirked before flipping Natasha over.

Leaning over her, he nipped one ear. "I assume at least one of those other tattoos is on your back."

Lifting her head, Natasha kissed him and bit his lip lightly before raising and eyebrow. "I never knew you were so turned on by ink."

"I didn't either, until I found out about yours." Her moan

pressed against him, and he forced himself to focus as lust radiated through him.

Her hand reached back, stroking him. "Yoga has made me very bendy."

"So I see." He shouldn't be able to get hard again so fast, but this was Nat. And she was all he needed. Grabbing her wrist, he pinned it by her head.

Lifting her butt, she pressed against his erection. "Finnegan."

"I promise," he offered, caressing the inside of her wrist with is fingers, "that I will make you scream with ecstasy, but first I plan to worship every inch of you."

A bright green tractor covered her right shoulder. The tires had small hearts cut out and the phrase, *there's no place like home,* steamed out the top. It was so Natasha.

Moving his hands lower, he slipped his fingers between her legs still wet with their first coupling. Skimming her delicate nub of pleasure, he stoked the bud, enjoying the moans she was attempting to bury in her pillow. "Finding out what other images you had on your body has kept me awake for weeks." Thrusting a long finger deep into the wet heat of her body, Finn continued, "Now, my fantasies will be accurate."

Rising against his hand, Natasha's body moved in rhythm with his stroking finger. "I have one on my inner thigh, too."

"Perfect," Finn murmured as he kissed the divot between her buttocks. Placing his hand on her hips, he guided her body as she languidly rolled over for him.

"I could get used to this worship," Natasha whispered as he ran his tongue down her belly.

Trying to ignore his torturous need to bury his length deep inside her, he spread her legs and stared at the compass wrapped around a lily. The words, *Not all those who wander are lost,* was written in delicate script against her skin. Skimming his hand across the design, he bent his head and nipped at the delicate skin. Kissing the inside of her thigh, he moved slowly towards the inner sanctum calling him.

Natasha's pleas had long since turned into low moans. Suckling her, Finn relished the sounds of her need. The lift of her thighs. The pressure that built only for them.

Pulling at his hair, Natasha forced him to lift his head. Her eyes were dilated with pleasure, and she shifted to capture his mouth. Surprising him, she pushed him onto his stomach, grabbed a condom from her top drawer, straddled him, slipped the condom on, and joined them. "I've waited long enough for you, Finn."

Leisurely moving her hips, she ground against his acceptance. Raking her fingernails across his chest, she swirled a finger around a nipple before bending her head to suckle the raised bud. Rising and then easing back onto him all the way drew a hiss from his lips. If she was trying to drive him to oblivion, it was working.

"Honey. Please."

Her eyes glowed as Natasha moved with intention. "I needed you."

Those words nearly broke him. But he was not losing himself until she was satisfied.

"Nat!" Finn caught her mouth as she drove them over the edge.

Chapter Eleven

REACHING over to silence the buzz of his watch, Finn stared at the mess of crimson hair cascading around the pillow. Careful not to wake her, he traced the line of freckles down her nose. They looked softer in the morning light, not yet sun kissed. It made her look like the young girl he fell in love with all those years ago.

How had he stayed away? He should be flogged for such stubbornness.

Natasha snorted, and he had to keep from laughing. No doubt she would agree with his assessment, if she were awake.

"I'm not staying away anymore, honey. I hope you're ready to be stuck with me," he whispered. She smiled but didn't wake up.

Carefully sliding from the bed, Finn went in search of a caffeine fix. Her home wasn't large, but it felt nice. His place in California had a sterile feel because he was hardly ever there. Natasha's apartment felt lived in. The comfortable feeling of knowing you are in a safe space.

Natasha's kitchen was small but clean. Her coffee pot sat next to the oven, and a part of him almost jumped with excitement. He tried to give it up once. His assistant, Katiya, and four of his engineers threatened to quit. If he'd didn't either take two weeks off to deal with the withdrawal symptoms or drink the coffee Katiya held. He started the pot and took his first sip before the brew was done.

As much as he longed to wake Natasha up with a mug of coffee and his lips, she deserved to sleep in. Downing the cup, he poured himself another round and was startled to hear scuffling by the front door. Moving swiftly, he opened it before considering that answering the door in boxers may be cause for talk. That thought fled as he saw Brad stand after laying a bouquet of daisies down.

"Just so you know, that's her least favorite flower." Finn smirked as he took a sip of coffee and tried to contain his anger. Answering the door in his boxers was bad enough to fill the town gossip cannon fodder coffers. Leaving the former "star" quarterback with a black eye wouldn't help matters. No matter how sleazy Finn suspected Brad might be.

"Guess I know why you stood up for her character," Brad sneered, as he grabbed his wilted flowers.

Cocking his head to the side, Finn tried to figure out the best way to handle this awkward situation before Natasha woke. "An interesting statement coming from a man attempting to woo my fiancée. If you think her character is so lacking, I wonder why you are bothering to bring her flowers."

Brad stormed towards the street without answering. A few daisies slid from their loose wrapping. The sidewalk was going to be covered in stepped on daisies.

"She loves me, she loves me not," Finn hummed as he closed the door.

He'd called Nat his fiancée. That was a mistake. If Natasha heard he'd called her that, she might flee this adventure. He wouldn't lose her again. She was going to be Mrs. Matus again, and this time, he was definitely attending the ceremony.

Pushing thoughts of Finn out of her mind, Natasha pulled herself from the car. For the last week she'd woken in his arms, and she hoped he'd be by her place later this evening. A beep on her phone sent her heart racing and crashing as a text message from her friend Scarlett stood at the top of her notifications.

She needed to gain control of herself. Finn had been at her place each evening, and they'd had fun. They never talked about the future, though. Never spoke of the business adventure he was planning.

Standing at the door, Natasha paused, enjoying the tantalizing scent wafting from her neighbor's side of the duplex. Her stomach grumbled with envy. No doubt a gourmet spread was being laid for someone very special. Mrs. Yeager only hosted her book club or prayer group. Two groups, to which Natasha had a standing invitation. However, usually it was a light, cheese spread and some chocolate chip cookies served at those events. For a moment, Natasha considered knocking to say good evening. Perhaps her friend would take pity on her and invite her to stay for dinner.

Focusing for one more moment on the closed door leading to Mrs. Yeager's sanctuary, she elected to open her own door. Her planned ham and cheese sandwich seemed decidedly unappetizing. Sliding the key into the lock, she promised herself for the millionth time she'd sign up for a cooking class. "Or at least borrow a cookbook from the library."

"Do you always talk to yourself when you arrive home?" Finn looked up from setting the table and smiled at her shocked expression.

Rather than answer, she returned his smile and accepted a quick peck on her cheek. "My apron looks great on you."

Finn glanced at the yellow ruffles and pulled a bottle opener from the large sunflower pocket. "Do you mind? It looked brand new."

"Not new, just unused," she stuck her tongue out as he tried, and failed to conceal a smirk. His attempt at diplomacy was sweet, but the fact that she had no aptitude in the kitchen was hardly a secret. "When I told you the location of my spare key this morning, I didn't expect to find you cooking me dinner. Though, I admit it's a delightful surprise. I thought Mrs. Yeager was cooking. I almost tried to invite myself to dinner."

She crossed her arms as his laughter reverberated off the walls, "I fail to see how that is so funny. I may not enjoy cooking, but that is hardly a crime."

With his shoulders still shaking, Finn pulled her into his arms. Pushing a strand of red hair behind her ear, he lightly kissed her cheek. Strong hands moved slowly across her back, and she failed to hold back a groan as his lips brushed hers. "I'm not laughing at you, sweetheart."

"Felt like it," she muttered.

"My apologies," Finn traced light kisses down her neck. "Mrs. Yeager was here about fifteen minutes before you arrived home, clearly looking for a dinner invitation." Finn's hands tightened on her, as she moved to step away. "I gave her dinner and dessert."

His phone buzzed, and Finn frowned.

"Everything okay?" Natasha kissed his cheek. Finn's phone had been ringing throughout the last several days, yet he never answered it in her presence.

"Just another job offer." Finn glanced at the message before holding up his phone and making a show of turning it off. "Nothing is getting in the way of our dinner."

"How many offers have you gotten?" Natasha's lungs

were hot. How many people were trying to pull him away from Walkins? From her.

"It's standard after an acquisition," Finn shrugged.

He hadn't answered her question. Did he think she'd insist he stay? Nat wanted him in Walkins but loving someone meant encouraging their dreams. She was not going to demand more than he could give. Placing a quick kiss to his lips and then purposefully heading up to her bedroom, she called. "I need to change."

"Want to postpone dinner?" Natasha winked, but her body cooled as Finn shook his head.

"We need to talk first." The sudden serious tone of his voice sent chills down her spine as she headed to her room.

Finn followed her, placing a kiss on her naked shoulder. His finger skimmed her stomach before he stepped back. Keeping her back to him, she focused on steading her breathing. Had he accepted a job offer?

You're jumping to conclusions. Don't be an idiot. I'm not.

The warring thoughts tumbled through her. Breathe. She just needed to breathe.

"Honey?"

She failed to control the flinch as Finn spun her to face him. "If you've accepted a position in California, you can just tell me. There was no need to cook me a fancy dinner."

This was fine. It was. She expected it. She could handle it.

Rather than step away, he grabbed both her hands. "I have not accepted a position in California. I know you have little reason to trust that, but I swear, I'm *not* leaving Walkins without telling you." Pursing his lips, he shook his head before placing light kisses across her knuckles. "I came across some information regarding the bitcoin hack and wanted to share it with you."

He's not leaving. Her heart crowed. *At least not yet.*

The beat of her heart steadied. She quickly put on some

comfy clothes then, tilting her head to the side, she placed a chaste kiss on his cheek. "Sorry, I shouldn't have assumed."

She swallowed as Finn kissed her forehead. "Nat, there are going to be no surprise disappearances. No, it was great seeing you, but I have to run this new startup. Promise."

Natasha wanted to believe him, but his eyes gleamed when he said the word startup. Finn loved running a business and eventually, it would call to him. Kissing his cheek, again, she made for the kitchen. "Dinner smells great. You can tell me whatever it is over a massive plate of?"

"Chicken tacos with chili guacamole and pineapple upside down cake."

His hand itched to fill his wineglass to give himself a few more moments to gather his thoughts. They'd kept to mundane pleasantries throughout dinner and dessert, but silence enveloped them. Empty dishes sat on the table as Natasha lifted her wineglass.

"How much do you know about computers?" He'd started his well-rehearsed script three lines in and watched Natasha's understandable confusion. He was making an accusation, and in a small town, that was no minor thing.

Shrugging her shoulders, her auburn hair drifted across her eyes as she tilted her head back and forth. "I can run the company's accounting records and maintain business documents. I know how to use search engines, run social media ads for the company and maintain the company website. However, I don't know how all the code works. Do you think I need to hire an IT specialist?"

"Yes. Given your expansion plans, you'll need an entire department, but that is a discussion for another day." Her nose twitched, and he pushed on before she could change the conversation to her well-developed plans.

There was no good way to drop bad news. "Someone in Walkins hacked your system."

"You're sure?" Nat started collecting the dishes. A college professor in one of the electives he'd taken talked about how some people, particularly women, cleaned or did menial tasks after hearing bad news. It was a defense mechanism to control the here and now. Betrayal was hard. Her hands were shaking, and he worried she'd drop them.

"Nat, let me do that."

"I should do the dishes, you cooked." Nat's voice was soft, distant.

"I cook. You clean. A great deal, but not tonight. Let me take care of you." Natasha nodded in agreement as she slid back into her seat.

Warm water fell over his hands as he looked over his shoulder. She was so still. No tears. No anger. Those emotions would come when the shock wore off. He'd known the news would upset her, but she needed to understand that it hadn't been a random hack.

A few minutes later, she wandered over to him. Light fingers trailed along his back before Nat grabbed a clean plate and started drying. "How do you know it's someone in town?"

Leaning over to kiss her cheek, he reveled in the domestic moment before turning to business. "I had my IT department look. It wasn't a sophisticated hack, at least not to trace. Eli believes the culprit bought the script that locked your computer. Probably sent it to someone in an email. Once it was opened, the code downloaded and boom."

"You can buy a computer virus?" The damp towel slapped down on the kitchen counter flipping two clean plates to the floor. "Damn it."

Finn shifted, lifting Natasha up on the counter.

She frowned, "I can clean up broken glass, Finn."

Raising her bare feet, he stared at her. "I know you are

capable of anything. At least let me clean a path, so you don't cut the bottom of your feet."

She crossed her arms but stayed put as he disposed of the dangerous mess. She was frustrated and taking it out on him. He understood. Hell, he'd done far worse when he'd arrived in town.

"You can purchase just about anything on the internet. For all the wonderful innovations it has brought, it can be a dark place." He dumped the glass in the trash and turned back to her. "Do you have any idea who might wish Saddler's ill? Any disgruntled employees, angry suppliers, or discarded boyfriends?" He leaned against the counter, holding her as she lay her head against him. She tensed, and Finn wished there was a way to wipe the hurt away with a few taps on a keyboard. But it wasn't that simple.

Soft fingers ruffled his hair, and she kissed him before leaning back against the cabinets. "We've fired a few employees and changed suppliers before, but nothing in the last few years. The only ex I have with any computer knowledge is currently staring down my shirt. Don't think I didn't notice," she laughed, as Finn traced the top of her collar. "Unfortunately, that narrows our suspect list very little. What do I do?"

"Tomorrow, file a report with the police. I have the documents showing the transactions, so I suspect they'll need your laptop." He lifted her from the counter and pulled her to him.

Her stomach was warm as he slid his hands under her shirt before lifting it over her shoulders. "Tonight, you make love to me."

Her tongue darted across the hollow between his neck and shoulder before she raised his shirt. Her shorts fell to the floor, and he shuddered as her fingers skimmed across the top of his jeans. Nat wrapped her legs around him as he carried her to the kitchen table. Deftly, Finn freed her breasts from her silky red bra.

"You are so perfect," he purred as his lips lowered to suckle a raised, pink bud. He could worship her breasts for hours, days, and not feel satisfied. Insistent moans filled the kitchen as he moved his mouth slowly towards the other breast. Natasha's back bowed, and she circled his hips with her legs, pulling him closer to rub her body against the bulge of his erection.

"Finn."

Kneeling, he nipped at the inside of Natasha's thigh. His tongue lightly licked the points of the compass. Teasing his finger up towards her center, Finn licked his way across her thighs, reveling in the rising desperation of her cries. Kissing his way up her body before standing to unfasten his pants, Finn teased his fingers across her belly before dipping ever lower to the place he knew she craved. Not allowing him to claim her, Natasha slid off the table and to her knees.

"Two can play games, Finnegan." Her nails sank into his butt as her lips traced the top of his erect shaft.

"Nat," he groaned as her tongue slid down his length. Her hand cupped him, and he rested his palm against the top of her head. *I wanted, needed—*

Before he could finish the thought, Natasha claimed him, and the warm wet musings of her mouth engulfed him. She wasn't demanding while coaxing his desire out by stretches and pulling him almost to the edge of completion before slowing.

It wasn't enough. He needed all of her. Finn turned her away, smiling as she laid her body against the kitchen table and opened her legs. He needed her but wasn't rushing this. He grabbed the condom he'd taken to carrying in his back pocket, since they'd reconnected, and slipped it down his length.

Then, he pushed into her. Slowly. Millimeter by millimeter. Nipping the back of her shoulder, he withdrew before pressing against her again.

"Finn, please," Natasha begged, as she turned her head to look at him.

"I thought we were going slow." He pushed a little more towards her center.

Her breath hitched. Arching her back, Nat growled at him, "Finnegan."

He almost gave in but pulled back slightly to move his hand around her tight ass and press a thumb against her nub. Circling the tight bud, he pressed into her before filling her completely. It took most of his control to repeat the process, but the sound of Natasha's panting breaths drove him.

"Finnegan, now, please."

Giving into her demands, Finn braced their bodies against the table. He drove himself to the hilt, once, twice, and cried out as Natasha's body convulsed around him on the third.

Detective Scarlett Blist tapped her pencil against the small pad she always kept in her suit jacket. Her friend promoted to detective a year ago, but Natasha still found it weird to see Scarlett dressed in a suit rather than police blues.

"Since we are talking actual police business, am I supposed to refer to you as Detective Blist or just Scarlett?" Natasha fidgeted in her chair and rearranged the cup of pencils on the edge of her desk.

"Scarlett works fine, Natasha. We are just having a discussion regarding the issues that occurred with your computer. Relax." Scarlett's curly, dark hair bobbed as she looked up from the notes, she must have taken over the phone this morning. Her light purple blouse looked amazing against her dark skin, but her eyes were a little haunted.

"Are you doing okay, Scarlett?" Natasha regretted the words as soon as they escaped. Scarlett was going through more than a rough patch with her husband. Her soon-to-be-ex-husband. She wasn't fine, and everyone knew it.

Her friend's lips tightened, and she refocused on her notes. "I'm on duty, Natasha. Some night, we'll go out and drink to your late husband and my asshole, but today we need to focus on the issue at hand."

Natasha's cheeks burned, but she understood. Scarlett's husband had not been discreet when he decided to step out on their union less than a year after they took their vows.

"So, Finn found the hacker?" Scarlett's tone was professional and clipped.

Pinching her nose, Natasha felt lost. "I don't think that's what happened. I think he tracked the hacker here, but I'm not completely sure how."

A phone buzzed in Scarlett's pocket, and her friend nodded before stepping out of Nat's office. She should have asked Finn to attend this meeting, but this was Saddler's' business and that meant Nat needed to do this on her own. That pride seemed hardly worth it as she stared at the limited notes she'd made after dinner last night.

"I need to go. I can come back later to follow up. Our department doesn't have the resources to track cyber issues. If you lost a sizable amount of data or money, the FBI might be able to help. I can give you the contact information for the Landers' office, or I can find the number for their main office in Cheyenne. Unfortunately, I don't have contacts there."

Scarlett moved to shake Natasha's hand, and she glared at her friend. "On duty or not, we are hugging." She pulled Scarlett into her arms. Her friend relaxed a little before she stepped away.

A knock at her office door made Natasha look away, and Scarlett said, "You have another visitor. We will go out sometime soon."

"See you later," Natasha called as her friend dashed

passed Brad. He loomed in the doorway, and Scarlett had to squeeze past him. *Jerk.*

Plastering a smile across her face, Natasha directed her attention to him and indicated he was free to take the seat Scarlett had vacated. Whatever he wanted, she hoped it was quick. Brad took command of the chair while staring at Natasha. His gaze roamed over her, and she lifted her eyebrow but didn't ask his purpose.

In high school, Brad enjoyed being the center of attention. As the star athlete things were given to him. Girls, grades, and gifts had fallen into his possession. Excuses easily generated for his poor academic and behavior record. Those adolescent passes resulted in an adult who believed he owned the world or at least should. She had things to do, but she did not start the conversation. A petty part of her didn't want to give into this game.

A flush passed over his cheeks as he realized that she was not going to ask his purpose. Brad narrowed his eyes before grinning through thin lips. A light chuckle rose from his chest as he leaned forward and invaded the space she placed between them. "Everyone thought Finn was the smart one, the brilliant one."

"Do you need something, Brad, or are you here to be an ass?" Finn was a genius, and he tutored Natasha through high school and college. He never made her feel dumb for taking longer to read through an essay or to write a paper. None of that should matter to Brad.

"But," her skin crawled as Brad leered, starting right back up where she interrupted, "you used your own wiles for advancement, haven't you, Nat?"

"Get out. I will not take whatever this is. You aren't Saddler's insurance provider, and we aren't interested in anything you're offering." She stood, pointing to the door.

Brad crossed one leg over the other, ignoring her order. "I

registered a fraud complaint against you and Warren's estate."

The words were so weird she suspected she misunderstood. She crossed her arms. She was not extending whatever fantasy this was. "His farm had no policies with your firm. Warren used Mr. McCormick. The policies have already been paid out to the estate. Not sure what game you're playing but it's *not* funny."

Brad stood and grabbed her wrist. "You might want to hear me out. After all, we wouldn't want the town knowing the darling of Walkins is guilty of insurance fraud."

His stale breath invaded her space. Pulling her arm away, she stepped back, refusing to look away from his angry stare. "Explain and then get the hell out of my store."

She did not move. He was not welcome here, and she wasn't going to extend this by sitting down. Brad scoffed as he focused on removing a small piece of lint from his shirt. "Warren had a longstanding policy with our office. You are to receive almost a quarter of a million dollars as his surviving spouse."

The air rushed out of Natasha's lungs. Maybe she should have returned to her chair. "No. That isn't possible. I knew nothing about it."

"Sure, you didn't. You married a sick, old man out of the goodness of your heart. Little Natasha Saddler, savior of Walkins." Brad scoffed before continuing, "I am sure several women would have married him and put up with his marital attentions for so much cash."

Her stomach rolled. That insinuation diminished the relationship she and Warren shared. "I knew nothing about that policy. So, there is no way to hold me responsible for fraud. You're grasping at straws and punishing me for." Natasha ran her hands through her hair, then stared at him. None of this made sense. They'd been on a single date and, while not friends, had always been polite.

"I don't know why you are saying such things, and I don't care. My reasons for marrying Warren are my own. I will thank you to leave my store now," she raised her voice and opened the door to the office.

"Of course, what's two-hundred-and-fifty thousand dollars, when you can have his filthy rich nephew?"

Blood drained from her face, but she didn't meet his gaze. "Excuse me?"

"Rumors have it that he didn't take long to crawl back into your bed. I saw him at your place when I came by a few mornings ago to have this conversation in private."

She fought to control herself. *Why hadn't Finn told her about Brad's visit?*

Brad's eyes roamed to her breasts. This was over. Her fingers flexed, and Brad's gaze shifted to her fist. For a moment, she suspected he wanted her to hit him, and that was enough to cool her actions. "Good day, Mr. Cross."

Chapter Twelve

Light buzzed across Saddler's as Finn stepped through the front door. Nerves and fear skittered across his belly. Nat worked the morning shift, but it wasn't her Finn was seeking tonight.

"We're closed," Herb's voice called from the back.

"This place needs to learn to lock the door at closing time," Finn joked and watched Herb's lips twitch before his eyes settled into a steely determination. "Glad to see you up and working again. I thought maybe we should talk?"

"About your offer to purchase my share of the store? I haven't made my decision," Herb's tone stayed professional, but Finn heard the hint of uncertainty laced beneath it.

He hoped Herb would sell his share of Saddler's to Nat, but if he didn't, she would not lose it to a stranger. "No, I want to talk to you about your daughter, and the fact that I'm going to marry her."

"I seem to remember already *giving* you my blessing." His words were flat.

"I kind of figured that blessing might need to be renewed." Finn's attempt at levity backfired as Herb glared at him.

Crossing his arms, Natasha's father pulled to his full height. Finn had about an inch and a half on Herb, but that didn't mean the man wasn't imposing.

Holding his palms out, Finn took a deep breath, "I never stopped loving her, sir."

Herb ran his tongue over his teeth before leaning against the counter. "You have a funny way of showing it, son."

Herb hadn't told Finn to get the hell out, which was good, because Finn wasn't capable of staying away from Nat. Not anymore. "I can't apologize enough."

"Have you apologized to her?"

It was a simple question but loaded. "Yes, for many things."

"If you hurt her again, I will hunt you down." He tilted his chin up. This was no idle threat.

"You'll have to get in line. Several people have threatened me." Finn answered with no trace of hurt or anger. Nat was loved. That was more important than his pride over the choice he made in the past.

"You weren't here to see the damage." Herb's shoulders sank as he blew out a breath and took a long look at Finn before continuing. "It was bad, but it took us all a while to notice."

"Why?" These were words Finn needed to hear, even knowing how much they'd hurt.

Herb's eyes wandered for a few moments. His cheeks flushed, and then he met Finn's gaze, "She never cried, at least not in front of anyone. She put on this happy, false smile, telling everyone how proud she was of you for chasing your dreams. How she expected you to make it big, and eventually, the Welcome to Walkins sign would read, Hometown of Finnegan Matus. I fell for the lie."

Moving to lock the door, Herb motioned for Finn to start with the cleanup. They worked through the subtle harmony of cleaning routines and the closing checklist. Finn refused to press for the memories that clogged Herb's face. Eventually, he continued, "It took me almost a year to see through her charade."

Finn looked up from wiping the counter, and Herb leaned against the broom. "She didn't stop moving ever, and she still doesn't. She found a task, completed it and moved onto the next thing. Always giving one-hundred-and-ten percent, and she hasn't slept well since you left. It took me a year to figure out you two had been sleeping together."

Fire flared across his cheeks, and Finn didn't know how to answer. They'd been young and in love. It wasn't a topic he knew how to discuss with the man he hoped would be his future father-in-law.

Luckily, Herb spared Finn but only just.

"I don't mean sex, Finn. I'm not naïve. You were young adults but adults. She needed you to sleep. Her mother and I were married for forty-two years before I lost her." Herb's voice shook a little, but he pressed on. "I understand needing your love next to you to rest. I suspect the small apartment she maintained off campus was for show."

Finn bit his lip and gazed at his feet. "Not really for show. I was her roommate, though my name wasn't on the lease."

"She told me she didn't sleep well because Warren needed medication every three hours." Finn felt hurt that she would have lied about such a thing, though at the time, she had little reason to tell him the truth.

Nodding, Herb looked at him with sympathy. "I'm not sure she realizes how tired she is. It's the reason I worry about letting her run everything. Her ideas are wonderful and, with a full-time partner who understands the modern economy, she's going to make this place truly something. Alone though, and I fear she'll put herself into the grave." Herb paused, his eyes shimmering before he added, "Her brothers. Caleb is on my side, but Liam thinks I'm being mean. He isn't on board with selling one of the family investments. Of course, he also hasn't offered to come home. She's been exhausted for years. Warren's illness simply exacerbated the issue."

"Nat and I are a lot alike." Finn shrugged. It was so easy to see when he looked at it. "I don't sleep in a proper bed unless I'm with her, or I didn't before I got home. For years, I figured it was because I was so busy with Reach. I slept on couches in the early startup days. There is a cot in my office, even in my home office."

Herb raised his eyebrow, "You two are a pair. When one goes missing, the other can be useful but never fully functional."

"I can't lose her again." Finn hoped Herb saw the sincerity running through him.

Thick arms encompassed him, and Finn embraced the scents of sawdust, smoke, and cleaner that felt like home. "You should have taken her with you."

"I thought her offer to run Saddler's was her way of saying Reach would never happen. I was so angry that the local investors told me no. When Nat offered an alternative, I saw it as a failure. It was childish. I cost us both time and love. I will never leave her again."

Slapping him on the back, Herb nodded to the door. "I'm not sure either of you would survive it, don't make me sorry for letting you date my daughter."

"I'm going to marry her."

"As soon as she tells me that, I will celebrate. Until then, goodnight, Finn."

Pulling up to Nightfall, Finn checked his phone again. Natasha hadn't texted to say she was on her way. He asked her to come straight from work, but she'd put him off. She needed to get a few things done and would let him know when she was on her way. In the end, that decision had worked out, and his talk with Herb had gone much better than he planned.

Stepping into the kitchen, Finn pulled on an apron and

checked the roasted chicken he started earlier. Depending on when Natasha would be here, he thought about making a batch of au gratin potatoes before settling on a cucumber salad. The back door opened as he slid the chicken from its roasting pan, and he grinned. "Honey, I'm in the kitchen."

Natasha stormed in throwing her purse on the table and glared at him.

"What's wrong?"

"Brad came to see me today." Her foot tapped against the linoleum. Her arms folded tightly against her chest. His Nat against the world.

Finn reached for her, but she stepped away and placed the table between them. "I will not have you plan my life, Finn. I enjoy the time we spend together, but, when you leave, I still need to live in this town. My reputation is important."

"I'm not leaving."

Flipping her hand to the side, she shrugged. "I know you're not leaving for the next few months, but I mean after that. When you pick a new company or start your own. Or whatever."

Pain twisted in his gut with the realization that she didn't consider this relationship permanent, but one issue at a time. With time she'd come to realize the truth of his words.

"What did Brad say?" He tried to keep the hatred from his voice, but the man deserved a broken nose for the callous statement he made the other morning.

"Why didn't you tell me he saw you leaving my apartment the other day?" Her voice was so high pitched that he flinched.

"I didn't see him as I was leaving. He came to the door, and I answered it—in my boxers, I should add. He had a bouquet and a box of donuts. He was less than pleased to see me."

Natasha's shoulders relaxed slightly. "Why would he have flowers and donuts?"

Finn suspected she spoke to herself, but the answer was easy to supply. "You are kind, smart, loving and drop dead gorgeous. Why wouldn't he be interested?"

She looked at him confused, "Our date was a disaster. I called him an arrogant jerk. I paid my half of the tab and stormed off. The only regret I have is that I didn't dump my drink down his shirt. The man didn't speak to me for almost a year, and I was fine with it."

"Okay. What are you actually mad about, honey?" Her eyes narrowed on the endearment. He lashed out at her several times, and he could handle her anger and frustration.

"You answered my door and never told me about the visitor. If I had answered the door, maybe Brad wouldn't." Tears choked whatever she might have said. Natasha crumbled into a chair and hit her fists against the table.

"How about we take a time out?" Finn offered and hoped she'd agree. It was a policy they'd instituted as freshman in high school. In those days, hormones collided into a few epic battles. Natasha had screamed timeout once, and it stuck.

"We haven't done that in years."

Grabbing for her hand, Finn gripped it. "We pause until dinner is finished. Then, we can give this argument more fuel."

Looking towards the oven, Natasha offered him a weak smile, "What's for dessert?"

Picking at the remains of her second piece of chocolate cake, Natasha's attempt to prolong the pause had maneuvered to the ridiculous. Her belly felt too full and her heart ached, knowing she had taken her anger out on Finn.

I'm trying to push him away.

Her brain repeated the thought throughout the comfort food marathon of roasted chicken, salad, and cake. She was terrified of living in Walkins, once he had no reason to return. That wasn't a good reason to go on the attack, especially when he wasn't the subject of her ire.

Staring at him, she gave a weak smile and launched herself into his arms. "I don't know what got into me."

Finn ran his thumb across her cheek. "You do. I am strong enough to hear it. Before you start though, you should know I talked to your father tonight."

"About?" She wondered how her father had reacted to Finn. He spent almost three years railing against the man until she told him to knock it off, or she wasn't coming to Thanksgiving. Her father had given in, but he was unlikely to ever be Finn's biggest cheerleader.

A soft kiss landed on the top of her forehead before he laid his head against hers. "I told him I was still in love with his daughter and was dating her."

She tensed, and he tightened his hug before dropping his arms. He gave her space to move away, if she wanted. It was the phrase she had longed to hear. The dream of him returning, begging her forgiveness and telling her he loved her. Her heart screamed for her to kiss him and make a fancy declaration, but her brain refused to let her utter the words.

He loved her before and left. His company was gone. His uncle was gone. She was the only link he had left. Today he might want to stay, but what happened in a few months? When he realized how tiny Walkins was, how little it offered compared to San Francisco? When a new company called with a fancy office and ridiculous sums of money? Her eyes darted to the door, and Finn moved aside.

"I won't stop you from leaving Natasha. However, I won't promise not to chase you, but I swear, I am not going to force you to utter the 'l-word.' That's not the way I want that phrase falling from your lips."

The door was ten steps from where she stood. She counted it out once, when she'd been up all night with Warren.

Ten steps to teach him what it felt like to be the one left behind.

She shuddered at the cruel thought. Then, purposefully, stepped back into his arms.

"I'm sorry." She didn't know if it was for her inability to say the words he longed for or something else, but she focused on the day's events for now. "Brad telling me I was under investigation for fraud has put me in a weird mood."

Finn squeezed her tightly. "I am going to kiss you, and then you are going to tell me exactly what that jerk did."

She started to protest, but his lips found hers and she lost the will to argue. He smelled of cooked sugar, flour, and a hint of mint. His stubble tickled her chin, as his lips grazed hers. Natasha moved to deepen the kiss, and Finn placed his hands on her hips, pushing her away.

"I want nothing more than to carry you upstairs and make you moan, and maybe scream, my name for the next hour, but I need to know what happened today."

She gave him a glare and then moved to the cupboard. If she was going to relive this afternoon, she needed a cup of tea. Before she could brew the water, two shot glasses landed in front of her, each with a finger of whiskey. Finn tipped his glass towards her and tossed it back. Natasha lifted her own glass, mimicking his motions.

The liquid burned beautifully as it slid into her belly. She wasn't alone. Finn promised not to push her, and he was here to help with her problems. Still, it felt awkward to unburden herself.

Leaning against the counter, Natasha relayed the entire story. Finn's face screwed through surprise and anger before finally landing on frustrated. She doubted it, but she finished by asking, "Do you know anything about this mystery policy?"

"Yes and no." Finn led her into the living room, and they settled into the couch. She leaned against him, enjoying the feeling of him running his hands through her hair. "I should have told you, but I thought he was just being a jerk."

Settling into his chest, she breathed a little easier as powerful hands caressed her back. She cringed as Finn related his meeting with Brad. The fact that the man had said such vile things. *And then* come to her place with flowers and donuts. At least her heart soared as he mentioned telling Brad about her character and ordering him to pay her.

Perhaps she'd actually get her happily ever after.

Natasha added, "Do you think there really is a policy? I didn't pay the company during the last year of Warren's life. I guess he could've paid ahead, but to be honest I'm not sure he was organized enough to think of it."

"He made you the beneficiary without telling you. I think it's possible he paid ahead on it to keep you from arguing with him about it."

"He was terminally ill, Finn. No insurance company is going to give a terminal man a huge policy. That's just bad business."

His arms closed around her, "If Brad is telling the truth, Warren had the policy since he took me in, so the company would be required to pay, despite the turn in his health."

"Do you think he can make the fraud charge stick? I didn't love your uncle."

Soft lips brushed across her ear, "You did, and it's okay to admit it. Perhaps not romantic love, but the tie was stronger than many marriages. I doubt he can do more than extend the time before you get paid."

Lifting her in his arms, he kissed her lips. "This is tomorrow's problem. Tonight, we are going to bed."

"You promised to make me scream your name, if I remember correctly." She yawned the last words.

Finn chuckled. "I'll collect another night. Tonight, we can sleep in each other's arms."

She laid her head against his chest. *I love you.*

Maybe tomorrow, she could gain the courage to say it aloud.

Chapter Thirteen

Leaning against her car, Natasha tried not to picture her truck sitting in the junkyard. It had been past time. She had gotten a good deal on the used Honda. Signed the papers this morning and said goodbye to the hunk of metal she knew the car dealer had no interest in.

And she still wasn't done with today's hard tasks. The large, red, brick building looked intimidating on the street corner. Natasha had never given the police station much thought, but today its imposing features seemed to dominate the small downtown area of Walkins. A few men dressed in blue exited the front door, but neither paid her any attention. She'd visited Scarlett a dozen plus times and never wavered on walking through the glass doors.

Grabbing her purse, she tried to clamp down on the anxiety pulsing through her. She was there to ask a few questions. Perhaps Scarlett would know a good criminal defense lawyer; Mark's expertise was purely civil.

You're getting ahead of yourself.

She took a deep breath as her stomach did its best to turn inside out.

No clutter covered Scarlett's desk, and Natasha admired

the crisp, clean organization of her friend's area. No matter how much she tried, her desk and general living space always seemed more lived in than organized. Not dirty, but more than one document had a coffee stain covering part of at least one corner.

"Natasha." Scarlett smiled, "This is a surprise."

She wished she had called ahead. Her mind had just sort of drifted to Scarlett without thinking. "Is there some place we can talk," Natasha kept her voice down to avoid drawing attention to herself. Brad must have reported her supposed offense to at least one of them and feared that someone thought her marriage to Warren was criminal made her sick.

Scarlett's mouth turned down, and the crinkles around her caramel eyes deepened before she led Natasha back towards an interview room. "Sorry, it's the only room we really have for private discussions. Tends to make people a little uncomfortable though."

"I should probably get used to it." Natasha groaned as she flopped into the chair.

Crossing her arms, Scarlett glared at her. "Why do you think you should get used to being in an interview room? Have you killed anyone lately?"

"No."

"Beaten someone up?"

"Of course not, Scarlett." She was just being ridiculous.

"Stolen a large sum of money."

"Maybe." The word was barely audible.

Scarlett sat down and reached for Natasha's hands. "Please don't take this the wrong way, but if you confess to a crime, I will have to take it seriously. Lauren may help you cover up facts, but I can't."

"Why would you say that? Lauren would never help me cover up anything."

"Ever asked her where she grew up? How she landed in Walkins? Anything about her past?" Scarlett held up a hand before Natasha could interrupt. "She is one of my best friends, too. I'm not saying she's a bad person, but she has a past that she's kept hidden for several years. She's running from something."

Sadness at Scarlett's assessment fluttered through her. Natasha made a mental note to ask Lauren a few questions. Just some pleasant, get-to-know you three years late questions. That wasn't her purpose today, though.

"Brad's accused me of insurance fraud." Natasha folded her hands in her lap. She waited for Scarlett to say something, but when she looked at her friend's face, it was blank. "Are you doing that thing they talk about on TV, where you wait for the suspect to fill in the noise? And now, I am filling in the noise."

Natasha clamped her lips closed and puffed air out her nose. She would not speak again until Scarlett said something. Scarlett pulled a notebook out of her back pocket and leaned forward. "First, Natasha, you are not a suspect. Next, I will tell you, as a friend, that if the insurance company has served you with papers, then they are contesting the payment of Warren's estate. Hence, you should seek legal counsel."

"No one's served any papers to me that I know of." Natasha twitched her head. "Brad came into the office to tell me I was under investigation. Most of the estate's been paid. I didn't know about this policy."

Scarlett scribbled a note down before biting her lip. "Natasha, I am having a little bit of difficulty following the line of your story."

Shrugging her shoulders, Natasha tried to explain. "Apparently, Warren had a whole life policy in effect since Finn was a child."

"Smart."

Nodding her head in agreement, Natasha rushed on, "I guess when Brad took over for Mr. Douglas, Warren's policy transferred to him. Anyways, Brad says I married Warren for the quarter million-dollar policy, and that he's investigating me. He also accused me of sleeping with Finn for more money."

"Brad referred to you as a gold digger, when informing you of his company's investigation?" Scarlett's voice echoed off the room's wall.

"I don't think he used that exact phase, but that was the gist of his accusation," Natasha conceded.

"Are you the beneficiary?" Scarlett was scribbling.

Natasha swallowed and tried to keep her nerves from exploding. "According to Brad. Finn and I have been looking for the policy for over a week. They'd scoured the estate each evening. They'd gone through box after box. Nothing.

"I could ask Brad?"

"Nope. No way." Scarlett snapped and then closed her notebook. "What I mean is, until someone serves you, formally, notifying you the company is challenging the will, I would not engage with Brad. Don't give him anything and hire a lawyer. I am certain Finn knows someone with knowledge of the field or has the resources to find the expert."

Her shoulders hunched under the weight of Scarlett's words. "I didn't know about the policy until Warren died. I might not have loved him in the traditional sense, but I cared about him and his health."

"What does love have to do with this?" Scarlett's dark gaze landed on her.

"That's Brad's argument. I wasn't in love with Warren. I must have married him for the money."

Scarlett's lips twisted into a half smile before she stood. "No company cares about love, Natasha. Hell, people marry for all sorts of reasons. I doubt Brad has any case. Still, get a lawyer and make Brad contact you through them."

She was on the sun-soaked street before Natasha thought to ask Scarlett why Brad might be vindictive regarding the policy, and then elected to drop it. She'd take Scarlett's advice, though. If Brad wanted to talk to her, he was doing it through a lawyer.

Someone knocked on her door, and Natasha looked up from her book. Pushing away her soup, she started for the door. The unappetizing meal was doing little to calm her nervous stomach. She wasn't expecting any visitors. Finn was in California for the week, and he used the spare key rather than knock.

"We know you're in there, Natasha."

Laughing, she reached for the knob. Lauren and Scarlett stood, decked out for the night. Grabbing her wrist, Scarlett pulled Natasha up the stairs as Lauren closed the front door.

"No sense in arguing. Scarlett wants to go dancing, and she's decided you and I are going with her." Lauren giggled as Scarlett headed for Natasha's bedroom.

"What if we don't want to go dancing?" Natasha crossed her arms, as Scarlett began rummaging through her closet.

"You *want* to go dancing. We all need to release some stress," Scarlett teased, tossing out a few low-cut shirts Natasha thought she discarded. "You just might not realize it until the music is moving through your body. Trust me. You both want to go dancing."

Scarlett poked her head out of the closet long enough to wink before diving back in. "You're in charge of shoes, Lauren. Something she can dance in."

"I think she needs to get out," Lauren whispered, as Natasha looked through the shirts Scarlett had tossed from her closet.

"Of course, I need to get out," Scarlett huffed, tossing a tight black miniskirt on the bed.

"I am not wearing that. The only time I did, it barely

covered my ass." Natasha reached for the garment, but Lauren lifted it first.

Why did she even still have that?

"I cannot imagine you in such a get up." Lauren held the barely-there fabric, placing it against her long legs.

Handing Natasha a tight denim skirt, Scarlett cocked an eyebrow at the miniskirt. "I'm surprised she hasn't gotten rid of her college clubbing gear, either."

Scarlett and Natasha had been friends since grade school, and Lauren had fit in from the moment she moved to town four years ago. There weren't a lot of single women above the age of twenty-five or below the age of sixty in Walkins.

"We used to dance the night away before we both married. Now, her husband is dead and mine is in Louisiana with his secretary. May she enjoy his dirty socks and cheating ways."

Scarlett let out a curse, then wrapped her arms around Nat. "I am sorry. I let my upset over this stupid day say something so equally stupid."

Natasha's face flamed. She hadn't even been thinking of Warren. And how had she forgotten what this week was? "I forgot your anniversary was this week. I am sorry, Scarlett. I have been so caught up in everything."

"You mean in Finn," Scarlett finished for her. Scarlett squeezed her tightly before stepping back. "My anniversary means nothing now. Finn's still not good enough for you," she added tapping Natasha's nose. "But if he makes you happy, that's all I care about. Plus, you promised me if he came back and broke your heart again, I would get to shoot him."

"What?" Lauren broke in.

"She's kidding," Natasha wasn't sure that was exactly the case, but Lauren looked a little relieved. "I don't think a detective is supposed to joke about that. Besides, I made that comment at twenty-three and very drunk. Finn and I are older. We enjoy each other's company, but that doesn't mean we're walking down the aisle."

"Right," Scarlett drew out the word as she peaked over her shoulder then turned back to the closet and pulled out a blue dress. "This was what I was looking for."

Rolling her eyes, Natasha grabbed the tight dress Scarlett had dragged out. She and Finn never discussed the future. It wasn't off topic. It just never came up.

Which basically means it's off topic.

"He still loves you, Natasha." Scarlett's voice carried through the bathroom door, as Natasha tried to figure out what to do with her hair. Pulling it into a slicked-back, high ponytail Natasha ignored the statement as she applied a light pink lip gloss.

"He does," Lauren chimed in. "Mark agrees."

Flinging open the door, Natasha pointed a finger at Lauren and raised an eyebrow. "Considering that Mark has loved you since the moment you walked into town, men in love may not be a conversation you want to encourage tonight."

Lauren's cheeks flamed as she headed towards Natasha's nightstand. "If you're wearing that dress, you need a necklace."

"Look who's trying to change the topic," Scarlett clucked.

"Mark is my friend. He's never indicated he wanted anymore." Lauren handed over a large, yellow flower necklace, dangling on a chunky chain.

"You take this one," Natasha passed it to Scarlett as the yellow always looked better against her midnight skin and went perfect with the purple ensemble she'd pulled together.

Grabbing the second necklace from Lauren's hands, she tied the white ribbon around her neck and adjusted the bright red apple charm. A bangle bracelet set off the final effect of her reflection in the mirror.

Finn would love this dress. Her friends were right, she was in deep.

———

Staring at the enticing image on his phone, Finn licked his lips. Natasha looked good enough to eat. After returning early, he went to Mark's after finding Natasha was out for the evening. He didn't begrudge her a girls' night, but he hoped she might go out with him dressed in that aqua sheath. He'd enjoy stripping it off her.

"What are you staring at?" Mark handed over a beer.

Passing the phone to his friend, Finn observed Mark's reaction. He bit his lip and followed the lines of the photo to where Lauren stood. "Any reason you haven't asked her out?"

"How do you know I haven't?" Mark tossed the phone and settled into the couch.

Finn studied his friend for a moment before answering. "You're still friends because you're scared, she'll turn you down."

Mark shrugged but didn't comment.

"You have to find a way to get over Tabitha." Finn regretted the statement.

Mark's jaw clenched, and he flipped the channel on the television. "Says the man who is doing his best to woo the fiancée he discarded more than a decade ago."

Glancing once more at Nat's picture, Finn tugged at his ear. "I did not discard her. I ran away." The results may have been the same, but the distinction mattered. "I'm attempting to convince her time, distance, and silence didn't change anything."

For me. The silent thought sent waves of panic through him. Natasha enjoyed their liaison, but she'd made no comment regarding the future of their relationship. He was so afraid of bringing the topic up. What if she bounced?

He was keeping his word not to pressure her, but it wasn't easy.

"What do you know about Brad Cross?"

Mark cocked his head at the shift in topic but permitted it by replying, "He's not much different now than he was in high school."

Pulling another sip from the beer, Finn asked, "Am I going to sound horrible if I say I don't remember him?"

Laughter filled the small living room, and Mark hit Finn across the back. "I should say yes because we graduated with less than fifty people. He was two, maybe three years ahead of us. Yes!"

Mark cheered as the hockey puck found its way to the back of the net. Trying to follow the game was a lost cause. Finn added, "How did you know him back then?"

"I played football and hockey, if you remember?" Mark answered without taking his eyes from the game. Lightly punching his old friend in the arm, he signaled Finn to grab and share a few more beers.

"I vaguely recall Natasha forcing me to attend some of those games. Supporting friends and school pride were her usual arguments, if I remember correctly." Twisting the cap off, Finn handed Mark the beer and raised an eyebrow, "Most people grow after high school graduation."

"Most do," Mark agreed. "Brad always wanted more than a small life in Walkins. He dreamed of an NFL career, but a college injury permanently sidelined him. At his best, he was backup material. Maybe. Don't tell him that. He has big dreams and no drive for success."

"He's wearing a three-thousand-dollar suit and six-hundred-dollar shoes." Finn laughed as Mark's beer went flying from his mouth.

"Who would spend that kind of money on clothes? More

importantly, how do you know how expensive his clothes are?"

Leaning his head back, Finn gave up any pretense of watching the game. "Seeing high-end designer digs is not unusual in the tech sector. For all the stereotypes of us in blue jeans and ratty nerd or band t-shirts, there is a ton of cash floating around."

"You're in blue jeans and a ratty shirt most days. I've seen press pictures. You're never in a suit." Mark sardonically looked at Finn's jeans and his plain, blue shirt. "Case and point, dude. When was the last time you spent cash on fashion yourself?"

"Hey! This is a nice t-shirt, no holes or anything." Playfully acting offended before returning to the somber discussion, Finn added, "Seriously though, lots of people drop a lot of income to achieve their version of the 'right' look. I'm just not sure why an insurance salesman in tiny Walkins, Wyoming is. Though if he has the money, who am I to judge? I'm just jealous because he wants to date my fiancée."

Mark's head snapped to attention, and then he cursed as cheering signaled the game's progress from the television. "Fiancée?"

"Don't tell Nat. I haven't run the idea passed her yet."

"You're playing a dangerous game, Finn. Nat won't be pressured into anything."

"I know." He wanted her whole heart, and he would not settle for anything less. "I never stopped loving her. I've done a piss-poor job of showing it, but if it takes years, I have every intention of making her my wife."

"Have you talked to her about your plans for Warren's ranch?"

Coughing as his beer slid down his throat, Finn took a minute before saying, "Not in depth."

"Now who's the worried one?" Mark's sarcasm rippled across the room.

Finn had surveyors out three times and hired a firm to draw up plans for two, small tech buildings. However, the zoning laws weren't changed, and there were still a hundred steps he needed to take to make his dream of an agricultural tech school in Walkins a reality. If it fell through, and he disappointed Nat? Well, he'd disappointed her enough.

Finn wanted to lay this project at her feet as a gift and proof that he believed in her dreams as much as she did. He had another secret too. "I may buy Herb's shares of Saddler's. At least I plan to, if her father sells his share after what happened."

"Talk to her about that?" Mark's voice was steady, but Finn felt the faint hint of threat behind it.

"Not yet. Her father promised to let me know if he plans to sell. He's convinced she needs a full-time partner, with or without him. I wouldn't bet against Nat, if I were him, but at least this way, she won't lose it to a stranger."

Keeping attuned to the television, Mark set his beer down, "I don't think she thought her father would actually be willing to part with Saddler's."

"I am not sure he would have before he had his health scare. I think since then, Herb has become terrified of Nat following his path." Finn understood it, but that wasn't a good reason to sell. "Then again, maybe he is tired of putting in those long hours himself?"

Mark confirmed, "Herb gave up a lot to run the store, even when she was younger. I think he doesn't want one of his children to do the same, and you might also be onto something about the greater joys of retirement."

"She's more than capable of running it alone, though."

"I don't think Herb worries about her capabilities, Finn. Natasha has an MBA and another degree in agriculture science. Sometimes, I think she fears being alone. It is almost like staying busy keeps her from focusing on that fear. Maybe that is part of the reason why she agreed to help Warren how she did?"

Focusing on being a bride left at the altar and widow before her thirty-fifth birthday were thoughts most people would run from, too. "Well, if Herb puts the store up for sale, I'll guarantee she won't lose the business."

Twisting his lips slowly, Finn tried to imagine Natasha's reaction. As much as he wanted to feel her jump in his arms, the reality risked being less kind. To his surprise, Mark bent over and laughed. Hardy chuckles, complete with tears streaming down his face.

"Glad to know my love life is so damn funny."

Attempting to catch a breath, Mark glanced at him and smiled. "It's hilarious, but I'm actually laughing at the fact that Warren was right. You two belong together, and it took him marrying Natasha for you to finally come home and figure it out."

"Warren told you that?"

Closing his eyes and holding his stomach, Mark tried to regain his control. "Yep, not long after their marriage. I asked if he'd bothered to ask your permission. He looked at me with glee. He said, once you found out, you'd be angry, and then you'd thank him for making sure she was off the marriage mart for a few months."

"Months?"

Mark's lips tightened, and his shoulders hunched slightly, "I don't think he expected his marriage to last more than a few weeks, to be honest. Then, Natasha found a clinical trial of some treatment and convinced him that, even if it didn't prolong his life, it might help someone else through the research gained with his participation." Mark paused before adding, "I think he'd have stepped aside as soon as you came home. He drew up divorce papers a week after they married, just in case Natasha changed her mind. I destroyed them when he passed as a testament to Natasha's willpower and care."

Gulping his beer, Finn stared at the window and tried to determine what emotions wrapped around him. Bitterness and jealousy warred for last place, as the feelings of love and compassion smothered anything else with appreciation. Tipping his bottle towards Mark, Finn toasted, "To Uncle Warren. The finest man I ever knew."

"To Warren," Mark responded before tipping his beer back and returning his focus to the third period. "If she doesn't kill you for buying her store, Natasha is going to make a beautiful bride. You better wear something other than blue jeans down the damned aisle."

"Thanks for going dancing with me ladies," Scarlett slurred as Natasha turned her friend's car into her small driveway. Her feet ached, but the dance floor had called her righteously. She needed a night to unwind, and Natasha never minded playing the role of designated driver. Leaning her head against Lauren, Scarlett let out a small cry. "I was a good wife, you know."

"Of course, you were," Lauren agreed as she patted Scarlett's head.

"Yet that didn't keep my husband from cheating on me. He told me that his mistress needed him. I apparently never did."

A small hiccup echoed from the back seat. Scarlett put on a good show following Doug's abandonment. Everyone has cracks, though. If she could reach out and touch Doug, Natasha would strangle the jerk.

Making low cooing noises, Lauren stroked Scarlett's hair. "Any man who doesn't relish the prospect of an independent wife, honestly, isn't worth our time.

However, being sad is okay, and it doesn't make you weak."

Nat helped Lauren get Scarlett into her house, into her pajamas, and tucked into bed. Then, they locked the door behind them as they left.

"Do you think she will be okay?" Natasha asked as they locked Scarlett's door.

"She's hurt, but she'll survive. It's just going to take time." Lauren wrapped her long arms around Natasha, squeezed gently before wrapping an arm around her waist, and lead Natasha towards her car.

"Do you think I'm a terrible person?" Natasha asked. The question slipped into the late night as Lauren pulled them to a stop.

Glaring at Natasha, Lauren challenged, "Why are you asking such a ridiculous thing?"

"Warren's been gone for only a few months, and I'm in love with Finn." Blowing out a sigh, Natasha climbed into the passenger door.

"If I died, would you ask such a question?"

"Are you feeling unwell?" Natasha heard the tension in her voice and tried to control the unexpected anxiety.

Lauren smiled. "No, but you loved Warren as a friend or an uncle at most. You had a modern-day marriage of convenience and largely for his benefit. Why should mourning him stop you from accepting the reality of loving someone else? You never stopped loving Finn. In a few months, Scarlett will realize she's better off without Doug. You never looked elsewhere for love, though. Why?"

Natasha remembered too late that starting a deep conversation with Lauren was always risky. The woman had a way of digging directly to the problem, whether you asked about it or not. "Do you believe in soulmates?"

"No."

She was a little surprised by Lauren's quick response but

pressed on, "Yeah, I didn't either, until Finn left. Part of me went missing. It sounds ridiculous, but it's the truth. When we are together, I feel complete. No one else has ever come close to making me feel that way."

Pulling her long hair from her ponytail, Natasha stared out at the passing cars. "I guess afterwards I was unwilling to settle for anything less than that feeling. Sounds stupid, I know."

Pulling up to the town home, Lauren let the car idle. "Not stupid, lucky. You are a grown woman, the only opinion that matters is the one looking at you in the mirror. You still love him."

"I do," Natasha kept her gaze focused on the door leading her to home, rather than meet Lauren's penetrating gaze. "What if he leaves me again?" Her greatest fear materialized in the darkness.

Some girls' night this ended up.

"Then Scarlett will get to shoot him, and I'll help you bury the body."

Despite herself, Natasha let out a laugh. "I might just take you up on that offer."

Chapter Fourteen

AFTER WEEKS OF FRUITLESS SEARCHES, Finn started to think any documents related to the mysterious insurance policy had been tossed for sure. Sighing, as he rifled through his uncle's farm desk, Finn tried not to curse the man. He'd never seen Warren sit here. He'd kept the beaten-up desk in the barn, mainly to dump old newspapers and random notes all over it.

Papers fell haphazardly around Finn, and he bent to grab the latest stack. Warren had given him back the woman he'd thought lost forever, but his organizational habits were abysmal.

Natasha had maintained archives of Warren's medical records. Every doctor's note and medical chart were recorded in neat penmanship, but she hadn't felt comfortable going through Warren's private records apparently. Finn didn't blame her, but if she'd looked, perhaps she would have found whatever insurance policy Brad said she'd used for fraud.

"This is ridiculous." Finn threw papers up in the air. Crisp, yellowed, shredded paper floated around him as he sat down on the ground. The faint scent of horse trailed along the room, and he frowned. A barn without a horse was a sad place. Once they sorted this ridiculous mess, he'd see about purchasing a few. Better yet, there were probably some rescues in the local area.

Beginning to gather the random mix of trash, Finn noticed a stack of papers laying under the desk. A simple note tacked to the top. 'Important.'

"I always put my important papers under the desk I never use," Finn muttered, hoping Warren's spirit was aware of the mess he caused. "Would it have killed you to put these somewhere, anywhere, she might have looked for them?"

Trudging towards the main house with his new find, he prayed there was something, anything of value. Groaning as a bill of sale for a horse in 1987 greeted him, Finn crumbled the paper and kept digging.

Slowly tracing through the mountain, he tried to see if there was any pattern. Under the bill of sale was a newspaper clipping announcing Finn's first software success. If he wasn't so frustrated, he'd be touched.

The wedding invitation for a long-gone event stared at him. Warren hadn't bothered to RSVP. The couple would be celebrating their second decade of wedded bliss in three months, if they were still together. Chucking the frilly mess, Finn leaned back in the chair and tried to think pleasant thoughts.

Towards the end of the pile, a wrinkled and coffee-stained document caught his eyes. The insurance policy was over two decades old, so he curtailed excitement. Likely, it was just an old policy on the barn, or even a long dead horse. His fingers trembled as he flipped through the first page. The whole life policy had been issued three weeks after Uncle Warren accepted custody of Finn with an addendum stapled to the back.

The change they'd been searching for!

Dated and notarized exactly one week after Warren married Natasha. Finn was long grown and no longer in need of a sizable policy. His uncle probably figured Natasha deserved it for all her help. He grabbed his phone and dialed Nat.

"Honey, I have great news!" This might not stop Brad's insinuation that Natasha had married Warren for the explicit purpose of inheriting, but at least now they had ammunition.

"That's the last of them." Finn's cheery tone sent a shiver of nervousness skittering through Natasha. "I'll admit, checking this off is an enormous relief before I head back to California tomorrow."

How did we clean the entire house so quickly?

Natasha nodded but said nothing. Dirty hands gripped her hips as Finn pulled her close, and she complained, "You're getting dust all over me."

Peppering her neck with light kisses, he nipped her skin. "Good now you have to shower with me."

"Will you be gone long?" She hadn't meant to ask that. Capturing his reply with her lips, Natasha deepened their kiss. Despite his declarations of love, she hadn't worked up the courage to say the same.

Finn pulled back and pushed a loose hair behind her ear. "I'll be back in a few days. The lawyers need me to sign some stuff for the sale, and I need to speak to my employees. Despite the weekly video conferences, I owe them a personal question-and-answer session. Though, what happens next really isn't up to me."

"Of course. So, about that shower?" The chirpy tone was too much.

Finn tilted his head, staring at her. "What's wrong, Nat? You've been distracted most of the day."

Bracing herself, Natasha took a deep breath, "Sorry, Finn."

"What exactly are you apologizing for?"

"For asking when you'd be back."

He crossed his arms and took a deep breath, but she saw the cord tensing in his neck. "You have every right to know when I will be back Nat. This is a relationship."

"Is it? What does that mean?" Fear drove those questions out of her mouth. Finn reached for her, and she collapsed against him.

"I'm not leaving you forever. Never again."

She kept her head buried in his chest, listening to the sounds of his heart. Strong hands rubbed across her back as he leaned his head against the top of hers. Her heart slowed in rhythm with his as her body relaxed into his heat. "I'm going to hold you to that, Finnegan. I spent days after you left pretending it was a mistake, and that you'd drive up tell me to pack my bag and come along. I want to believe."

Lifting her in his arms, Finn sat her on the counter and kissed her lips lightly. "Nat…"

Interrupting, Natasha kissed his forehead. "Everything worked out. You're a big rich technology guy, and I run a farm store."

"You run an impressive supply store that's expanding," Finn stated before addressing the larger issue. "Natasha, I understand fear. I know I hurt you, and that pain still haunts me. I thought you didn't want to come. That you thought I'd fail in California like I did here. It was immature, and it cost us both."

"Except you didn't fail, and you still didn't come for me." Natasha heard the pain in her voice, but, if she was going to give this a chance, she needed answers.

"I figured you hated me."

"People said I should," she lifted his chin and met his sad gaze.

"Maybe they were right."

Running her hands across the stubble growing on his cheek, Natasha gave him a weak smile. "I never hated you. I was hurt, confused and angry but hate was never in the cards. I never stopped loving you."

Finn's breath rushed out. She leaned in to kiss him as he whispered, "I love you, too."

As her lips parted, she pulled him closer to the point of almost sliding off the counter. Running hands through his dark brown hair, she pulled him closer for balance's sake. "What do you say, we get that shower?"

Curls of auburn hair fell across his chest as Finn opened his eyes. Gingerly, he reached for his phone while trying hard not to wake her. Natasha's soft snores echoed across the bedroom, and he watched her nose twitch as she turned against him. He should let her sleep, but if he was going to pull off his surprise before he had to leave for the airport, they needed to get moving.

"Honey." He rocked her shoulders, and she shot up. He grabbed her wrist and whispered her name until the sleep cobwebs vanished.

She shook her head, the curls bouncing as she turned to him, "Morning."

"I didn't mean to startle you."

She waved away the apology. "A force of habit. Maybe it'll go away, eventually, but at least I wake up fast." Stepping out of bed, she pulled on her blue jean skirt before rummaging through his closet. "I'm stealing a shirt."

Stepping up behind her, Finn trailed kisses down the freckles on her shoulder. "My closet is yours."

"Thanks, but if I'm going to keep spending the night, I should probably leave a few things here," she murmured as she pulled on an old flannel shirt.

He wanted her here every night. The idea of her clothes hanging next to his made his chest clench. When he returned,

Finn was going to ask her to be his forever. They'd lost enough time. "Bring whatever you want."

He kissed her lips before pulling her along. "I need coffee, Finnegan. I may wake up fast, but I still need caffeine."

The timer on the coffee maker dinged, and he grinned with satisfaction. After pouring her a cup, he grabbed her fingers. "Come on, I have a surprise I need you to see."

"That door leads to the garage, Finn," she grumbled as he opened the door.

"I know. Take a few more sips of coffee and trust me." He beckoned for her to follow him over the threshold. Oil and cleaning supply scents mingled in the air as they stepped onto the hard floor. Her truck, her ancient, beaten and battered truck, was parked in the primary space.

"I sold it for scrap," she whispered, running her hands along the fresh coat of blue paint.

"I was afraid you might not recognize it without the rust," Finn placed a soft kiss against her forehead. "I thought about getting a new bench, but I have fond memories of that seat, so I just had it reupholstered."

Her cheeks colored at his husky tone. "You fixed my truck."

She smiled and then burst into tears. Red eyes met his as she opened the driver's side door and clutched the keys to her chest. "This is the best gift."

Chuckling, he walked around and slid into the passenger seat. "It's got a new engine, new tires, and they stripped the rust and the radio will work. Though, I think most of what we used to listen to has been assigned to the oldies station. How is music from the nineties old?"

Interrupting his monologue, Natasha pressed her lips against his. Her floral scent intoxicated him as he ran his hands through her thick hair, pulling her onto his lap. In the tight confines of the truck's cab there was little room for her to do more than straddle his legs, but Finn didn't plan to complain.

Slipping a hand beneath the shirt she'd borrowed, he drew his fingers across her belly. Her breath hitched as she moved her tight ass against the bulge of his erection. Licking the divot at her collarbone, he winced as she leaned her head back and hit it against the top of the cab.

Natasha chuckled, "I think we are a little out of practice for making out in cars."

Kissing her, he let out a soft laugh, too. "We can go upstairs."

"Feeling too old to do it in my truck, Finnegan?" Need pulsed through him as she popped the top of his jeans and slowly inched his zipper down. Nipping at the base of his ear, her sweet breath rushed on, "The good thing about not having clothes stored here is that I'm sans panties under this skirt."

Lifting his hands away from her hips, Natasha purposefully slid them up her thighs. Her skin burned beneath his palm as she held his gaze. Dragging his fingers, he groaned as she placed his thumb against the pearl at the base of her mound. Finn couldn't look away as she slowly coaxed his hand to do her bidding. Using his other hand, he teased the buttons of her shirt open, kissing the freckled skin each new button revealed. Finn continued caressing her before gently sliding first one, then another, finger into her depths. Her body moved in rhythm as his fingers toyed with her. Natasha's groans filled the fogged cab as Finn refocused his attention on her breasts.

Pulling one shoulder of the shirt down, Finn used his teeth to release her crimson-tipped nipple from its lacy prison. Licking the first, he suckled and traced his teeth across the tip while enjoying the gasps of pleasure eliciting from the woman straddled across his lap. Twirling his tongue around the tight raised bud, he gently sucked, as she once more found his hard ridge and slid into his pants.

Her long fingers wrapped around his length. Finn gasped, "If you want me to last longer than I did the first time we were in this cab, I need you to stop."

Pulling her skirt over her hips, his breath hitched as Natasha turned around in his lap before sliding down him. Her body melted against his as she began to slowly ride him. Grabbing her wrist, Finn lowered her hand and followed her fingers as she began pleasuring herself. "God, Natasha," Finn moaned as her head fell against his shoulders. "I love you."

Eyes dilated with pleasure held his as she stroked herself, cresting into orgasm as she moved against him. Leaning forward, Natasha braced herself against him as she pulled her hair away from her face.

"I love you, Finnegan." Her voice lazy with passion, she moved against him, drawing out his pleasure. Natasha placed a feather kiss against his cheek. "We are taking my truck to the airport to drop you off, and when you get back, we'll find a nice out of the way parking spot to welcome you home."

"Yes, ma'am," he moaned as she slid off him.

Chapter Fifteen

Two pink lines confirmed Natasha's suspicions. Her upset stomach and random food aversions weren't going to abate anytime soon. Passing a hand over her belly, she felt fluttering joy mixed with panic. She went back on birth control after their first night against the wall. Obviously not soon enough.

How am I going to tell Finn?

She wanted him to choose her freely, not because of a baby. That was a worry for another day.

Natasha pressed a hand against her belly where a baby, no larger than a fingernail, grew. She was going to be a mom. A smile twitched and then bloomed. "Good morning, bean."

The happy phrase echoed through her as she readied for the day. Little reminders reinforced the news. Selecting decaf coffee, and the baby rejecting the sub sandwich she'd packed for lunch. Even her craving for ice cream, which logically she knew wasn't tied to the early pregnancy, but she planned to blame on the baby, anyway.

Her life was changing. It was scary and wonderful and tied into a loose bow. The only outstanding issue was telling her child's father. *He's going to be excited.*

No matter how she tried not to get her hopes up. It was

this thought that drifted with her anytime she thought of Finn's reaction.

"Natasha," an angry voice screamed from the front of Saddler's breaking her pleasant thoughts.

Racing towards the front of the store, she considered pressing the alarm but discarded the idea. No need to bother the police with an angry customer. It didn't happen often, and people sometimes overreacted to issues. In a small town, everyone knew the managers of local businesses. Amanda's eyes were wide as Natasha rounded the corner.

The young woman was pressed back against the counter, her face drained of any color. Her chocolate eyes met Natasha's, and she followed the young woman's gaze.

Brad stood by the front door. Why hadn't she recognized his screaming voice? Not that he looked like himself at all. His loose, blue jeans and long, sleeve t-shirt seemed so out of character she froze. Had she ever seen him without a suit? *Not the point right now.*

Her eyes went to the baseball bat. The one he was swinging freely. He narrowly missed the window. His eyes glowed with a desperate anger.

Aiming for control, Natasha smiled at Amanda, "Why don't you go see what is keeping Mr. Saddler?"

She opened her mouth and then blessedly shut it. Today was her father's day off, but Natasha prayed the girl would hit the distress button and then exit through the back door. Maybe she'd even pressed the alarm tied to the cash register. Nat couldn't count on that though. Amanda might have frozen when Brad started swinging the bat. But she knew the girl would call the authorities as soon as she was clear of the store at least.

The menacing giant stayed in place while Amanda rushed towards the back of the store. For a moment, Natasha worried he might react to her dismissal of the clerk, but his focus remained on her. Cocking his head to the side, he stared at her, saying nothing. Now that she was in his sights, the man seemed unable to determine his next path.

Swinging the bat again, Brad stumbled before regaining his balance. "You got what you wanted." His slurred words echoed in the silent store.

Raising her hands, she crept behind the cash register. The counter offered little protection, but it was better than standing in range of the bat. And it gave her the opportunity to press the alarm hidden under the counter. Couldn't hurt to have multiple alarms going off. Natasha tried to keep her voice calm. "I apologize, Brad, but I'm not sure what you mean."

If she could get him talking, it might buy her time while Amanda went for help.

Rolling his eyes, Brad once more swung the bat, again not at her. He was acting like a baseball player. "Calling the main insurance office in Cheyenne was a stroke of brilliance. They ordered me to release Warren's policy to you. No one wanted to listen to my arguments. They called me crazy."

"I'm sorry your company is forcing you to do something you don't want to." Annoyance burned through her as the words slipped through her lips. She didn't want to apologize for something that wasn't her fault, but Brad was already unhinged. "I didn't marry Warren for that policy, though."

"Sure," Brad mocked, "You married a sick, old man out of compassion. Then, why are you banging his rich, nephew months after your husband is in the ground?"

"My love life is *none* of your business." She had done nothing wrong. "I didn't know about the policy. I never even made a claim on it."

Sirens reached her ears, and she almost sagged against the counter.

Brad's eyes stalked across her, but his feet never moved. "You ruined my life."

If Natasha hadn't been so terrified, she might have

laughed at the ridiculous statement. "I went on a single date with you five years ago and have been nothing but neighborly since. I fail to see how you could blame me for any of the poor choices you've made."

Risking a glance out the window, Natasha sighed as the first police car pulled into the parking lot.

"This isn't over," Brad yelled as the first police officer raced in.

"I don't know what *this* is," Natasha whispered.

Her excitement at the authorities arrival evaporated as Brad pulled a pistol from the back of his waistband and ordered the officer to stay back.

The officer held up his hands and slowly retreated as Brad leveled the weapon towards her.

Breathe, Nat. Just breathe. She held her hands up, but he lowered the gun as soon as the officer was outside the store.

The store's phone rang.

"Pick it up and hang up." She did as he instructed. And pursed her lips as the phone immediately started ringing again.

"They're going to keep calling," Natasha sighed.

"Shut up." Brad ordered as he stared at the growing police arsenal outside the store. "This isn't how it was supposed to go."

He swung the bat, leaving a giant dent in the wood of her checkout counter. Natasha let out a cry but quickly regained her composure. She couldn't afford to upset him further. Another swing of the bat took out the row of fuel pumps from the sale shelf. Covering her ears, Natasha sank behind the cash register.

Leaning over the counter, Brad screamed. "I do not need to justify myself to anyone. I was the star football player of this piss-poor town. I should have been something. Instead, I'm a stupid insurance salesman."

Coughing, Natasha tried to keep from letting Brad's garlic

and booze infused breath make her lose her stomach. "What does that have to do with me?"

"Stand up, Natasha!"

"Okay." She did as he instructed but her brain was spinning. Why was he so pissed at her? She'd attended football games but never spent any time worshiping the players on the field.

He sneered and began pacing in front of her. "The life insurance policy Warren left. There is so much you could do with it. I planned to marry you, but you never gave me a chance."

"You said I was nothing special, and you acted like it on our date. Then, you hit on me at my husband's funeral." He glared at her, and Natasha flinched though his hands stayed by his sides. Arguing with a loose cannon was not a way to guarantee her or her child's safety.

"That was before you married Warren. I would have been different, if you'd said yes after he was in the ground."

Her head hurt from his lack of sense. "I can't believe you would want to be married to me."

"I have put up with being in this damn town for thirty-seven years, so I figured I could manage marriage to you for a few years or so. While we were married, I planned to get you to pay off my creditors, and if we divorced, I was banking on you being too sweet and stupid to request a pre-nup. When that didn't work." He lost whatever that train of thought as he noticed movement outside the windows of the store. He leaned back, pulling the handgun from his back waistband again. He flipped off the safety.

Goose pimples rose across her legs as she fought to keep a rational thought in her head. "Brad," she kept her tone level as he stared out the window.

He muttered to himself for several minutes before turning his attention back to her. "I'm still not sure how you got around the virus I emailed you. I thought you'd do anything to keep your precious store records. The man who sent it to me said it was foolproof. I just needed the money. All you had to do was pay the ransom!" he screamed.

His eyes squinted, and he raised the gun.

"Brad," she tried again. "You don't have to do this."

He glared at her, but whatever he planned to say was cut short as a bullet shattered the storefront. Natasha screamed, ducking to the floor. Footsteps pounded on the linoleum, but she didn't raise her head until she heard Scarlett calling for her.

Brakes squealing, Finn pulled into Saddler's parking lot and barely remembered to throw the car into park before running for the front door. He made it from the Cheyenne airport to Walkins in record time after getting Herb's call.

Please let her be okay, Finn sent the prayer to the universe for the millionth time in the last few hours.

"Sir, I need you to wait." The officer meant well, but Finn was terrified.

Brad was handcuffed to the bed being raised into an ambulance. His gaze landed on Finn, "Your precious Natasha is fine. My life is ruined, but what do you care!"

Finn ignored those words. He needed to see Nat. His heart wouldn't slow until he'd put his arms around her.

"Scarlett," he called, waving his arms, trying to catch her attention before she headed back inside. "I need to see her, please."

If she gave an indication that he was free to enter the scene, Finn missed it, but the uniform in front of him moved aside and let him pass. Briefly raising a hand in acknowledgment, Finn dashed for the door. Natasha sat on the checkout counter, feet swinging and looking calm but exhausted. The subtle shake of her hands was the only giveaway to the stress she was attempting to hide.

Sliding up, Finn hoisted himself onto the counter and felt her solid warmth next to him. Perhaps now, his heart could beat at a regular pace. His fingers ached to run across her body. He needed to confirm that she was uninjured. But this wasn't the time.

"I thought you didn't get home until tonight," she whispered as she laid her head against his shoulder.

"I caught an early flight. Your dad called just as I was landing."

"Sorry to worry you." She yawned.

"You are *not* apologizing for that ass's actions. I needed to see that you were okay. Although, I admit it's a small miracle that I made it here without getting a ticket." Lifting her chin, Finn lightly brushed a kiss against her lips.

"Excuse me," Scarlett's matter-of-fact tone interrupted them.

Natasha's cheeks were pink as she forced her gaze from Finn to her friend. He had no issue being caught kissing the woman in his arms.

"Did he threaten you with the bat or gun?"

Finn tensed at Scarlett's question and then moved to examine Natasha. "I didn't know he had weapons. That wasn't in the news report I heard on the radio."

"Finn, I need to ask the questions. Keep quiet or you'll have to wait outside." Scarlett's voice was straightforward and professional.

Natasha stroked his cheek, "I am fine, Finnegan. Promise. He swung the bat against the counter a few times, but not at me. He took out my fuel pumps," Natasha pointed to the mess on the floor before shuddering. "I didn't know about the gun until the first police car arrived. At first, it felt like he was showing off. Brad screamed at me a few times, but he only raised the gun at me once, at the end. I think he was drunk or maybe high. He acted weird. No doubt he's going to regret this decision tomorrow."

"I am not concerned about whether or not he feels sorry," Scarlett snapped.

Finn smiled. Her friend was trying quite hard to be the professional and not just kick Brad's ass. Natasha's shuddered, then took a deep breath. "Brad was ranting about me refusing to date him. I guess he wanted me to use the inheritance to get him out of some debt. It was odd and unfocused. He accused me of calling the main office in Cheyenne. He was angry they ordered him to pay me. That means they don't think I committed fraud? Which I didn't." Natasha hopped down from the counter and wrapped her arms around herself. She glanced at him. "Sorry. I can't stay still."

"You're fine, honey. Whatever you need to do."

"Neither of you called the Cheyenne office or committed fraud?" Scarlett asked.

Natasha rocked back on her heels. Finn hopped down and stood behind her, rubbing her shoulders. They were hard as rocks. Tension radiated through her, and she was very close to losing the control she barely maintained.

"Neither, Scarlett." She leaned back on him but was still stiff. "How many more questions do you have?"

Scarlett took a few notes and gave Natasha a tight smile. "I know it's hard, but if I treat this differently, his defense attorney might use that in court. I need to follow this one by the books, with no hint of friendly advantage."

"I understand. In a bigger town, you would have more than one detective on duty at a time." Natasha deflated against Finn.

"I called the Cheyenne office." Finn's head shot up as Herb Saddler walked calmly towards his daughter. Herb pulled Natasha towards him and hugged her tightly. Finn understood her father's need to touch his daughter and reassure himself that she was fine, but his arms felt empty. She stayed in her father's embrace for a minute before moving back against Finn.

"Is this a crime scene or not?" Scarlett looked over her shoulder at the deputy doing a lackluster job of keeping people out. "You called them, Herb? Why?"

"The fraud charge was ridiculous." Herb pulled a meaty hand across his face. "I assumed Brad was being petty. Everyone thought his actions at Warren's funeral were ridiculous. The Cheyenne office, though," Herb paused to wipe a tear away. "Well, they got fairly upset that someone was leveling a charge over loving your spouse."

"I'm surprised they were willing to tell you anything." Finn had wanted to help Natasha, too, but he'd assumed the insurance company might be unwilling to talk to someone other than Warren's next of kin—which was Natasha.

Herb glanced at Scarlett. "I might have insinuated I worked for the police department."

"I am going to pretend I didn't hear that." Scarlett flipped her notebook shut as she shot Herb a glare.

"I don't understand any of this," Natasha shook her head. Finn squeezed her shoulders as she added, "Brad's decisions make no sense."

"Criminals generally do things for one of two reasons. Love and money." Scoffing, Scarlett shook her head. "He is drowning in debt to legal, and illegal, creditors. The bank might foreclose his properties, but the mob will hurt him or maybe eventually kill him."

"Mob?" Finn clenched his jaw as the word slipped from his lips. Brad was involved with terrible people, and he'd wanted to drag Natasha into it.

"I started investigating him not long after Natasha came to me regarding the fraud case. Insurance fraud is a criminal offense. I waited a few days before discussing the subject with Brad, to see if he came to me first. When I talked to him, he clammed up and claimed Natasha was lying."

Natasha made an injured noise. "I wouldn't."

Scarlett nodded, "I know, Natasha, you are a terrible liar. We opened an initial case. I can't get into much of it, but suffice, to say he owes a lot of people money. Some of them are truly dangerous. I think he was aiming to find a way to claim your money as his own. I doubt he's been thinking clearly for a while. Terror causes people to do awful things. If I need more information, I'll call."

Scarlett pivoted and headed for the door.

"Sorry, Natasha. I really was just trying to help. No one likes to see someone take advantage of their daughter," Herb started once Scarlett was gone.

Stepping forward, Natasha placed a kiss against her father's wrinkled cheek and wrapped her arms around his sizable midriff. "Love you, Dad."

"Love you, too." Herb placed a kiss against the top of Natasha's head and then held Finn's gaze before leaving them alone.

"Ready to go? I think you've earned a full week off." Finn pulled her towards the door. She hesitated, and he leaned in, tasting her sweet lips. "What?"

"We aren't staying open, but Dad needed to talk to me. I was going to do it at dinner, but since he's here now," she bit her bottom lip. "I'll see you as soon as we're done. My place, cause I have no clean clothes at yours."

Only the fact that her father was standing so close kept him from saying he liked her with no clothes.

"And I wouldn't cry if you made dinner. I'm famished."

Finn pulled her in and kissed her deeply. "I'll have dinner on the table."

"I won't be long."

The florescent lights spun as she tried to process her father's words. She should have taken him up on his offer to discuss this later.

"I know it's been a long day, and I would have pushed this discussion if you hadn't been so stubborn." Her father pulled a hand across his face, "But I wanted you to hear it from me." His words sounded far away.

After everything, she'd lost the store.

"I had two offers, but one buyer gave us above my full asking price."

"Who?" Her words were quiet, as she lowered herself into the chair.

Side-stepping her question, her father prattled, "I entered a bidding war. Weird how exciting it was. I know that isn't important now. But maybe I'll get my realtor license when I retire."

Two offers. That couldn't be right. Her shell of a company had made their offer months ago when her father first put out feelers about selling. *No reason not to see the interest.* That had been his excuse when she'd pointed out that she wanted the store. She deserved Saddler's. All of it.

The commercial realtor promised to let them know if anyone else inquired. No. He could not be telling her this, not after the day she'd just had. He couldn't. This was too much. It was all too damn much.

She was furious, but she packed the anger away. Her body was drained of all the emotions it could handle. There'd be time enough to explode later. "And you didn't think to tell me you were finalizing a sale? I thought we would discuss any offers."

Her father reached for her, frowning as she stepped back. "Sweetheart, no offer was going to be good enough for you. Us arguing wouldn't have helped anything."

"Why would we argue?" Drawing in a ragged breath, she clenched her jaw. "After all, I'm the one who has been working here full-time, the one who wanted to run Saddler's and expand the business." Sobs threatened to overtake her as she stared at her father, "I am the one who has been planning and preparing."

"You can still do that. You'll just have a different partner, instead of me. A better partner," The door chimed, and her father frowned. People had been streaming in, looking for gossip regarding Brad's leap into criminality. "Should have locked that door an hour ago."

"Let the new management handle it. I'm off the clock." Natasha grabbed her purse. She needed dinner, sleep, and Finn. Not necessarily in that order.

She could smell the cookies Finn was baking before she opened the door of her apartment. She breathed a small sigh of relief. He was prepared with sugary treats, which was good since she couldn't drink away the day's sorrows.

"Natasha?" his voice made her smile as she threw down her purse.

"Nope. It's a robber, come to pilfer sweets." She tried to sound peppy, but as he rounded the corner she immediately fell in his arms. She lay against his white cotton shirt, inhaling the scent. She was here. Finn was here. Their child was here. Everything had shifted.

But some things hadn't.

The timer on the counter went off, "Do you need to get those?"

"Unless you want burned cookies, probably." He squeezed her but didn't let go. She got to make this choice.

"I've eaten burned cookies, but I don't really want to do it tonight." She gave him a quick peck on the cheek as she headed towards the plate of warm chocolate chip cookies he'd already put on the counter. She bit into one and moaned.

Nat wasn't exactly sure what it was about chocolate, but it elevated even the darkest moods. "Exactly what I needed today."

Keeping his back to her, Finn bent over to check on the cookies in the oven. "This batch still needs a few minutes."

She peered over his shoulder and frowned at the rising dough. She would never be a baker, but she loved his hobby. Picking up another cookie, she followed him to the small table.

"Your cupboards are always bare. This place constantly needs groceries. I keep home stocked, so maybe we should stay there a little more permanently?"

Natasha felt her heart lift at his casual use of the word home to describe Nightfall. "I wouldn't mind that. Particularly because it is out of town, and I can hide from dad there." She bit her lip. "He sold Saddler's. *That* was what he wanted to talk about. After I'd been held hostage for three hours. He sold it to some stranger. Without talking to me. Said he didn't want to argue."

"Not a stranger." Finn gripped her fingers and took a deep breath.

No.

"Honey, I bought Herb's shares of Saddler's. Not a stranger. You didn't lose it."

Her heart broke as he beamed with pride. Like this was a celebration. A win.

It's not as bad as it could be. That thought didn't provide much comfort though. Nat pulled her hand out of his, "You?"

"I started talking to Herb several weeks ago."

Weeks ago. Weeks ago. Without talking to her. No discussion of their future. No heads up. She panicked as a barely audible word left her mouth, "Leave."

Finn knew how much she wanted to do this on her own. Nat poured all her dreams out to him. He knew she wanted the store to herself. Knew what it meant to her. And he'd just bought it. Offered more than she could and stolen it.

Rationally she knew that wasn't fair. And if he'd talked to her. Planned with her. But no—he was building his own path without talking to her—again.

"Nat, just listen."

She shook her head. "There's nothing to listen to. You bought Dad's shares. You outbid—" Her throat seized. Finn was her partner. He'd invested in Saddler's. She'd wanted that so badly, but not this way.

Not behind her back. Saddler's was hers. Hers.

"I did it for you." Finn raked a hand through his dark hair, "Think about it. I can help you accomplish everything and more. We can expand outside Walkins, maybe outside Wyoming."

Outside of Walkins. Outside of Wyoming. Her heart collapsed in her chest. There was the real problem. Walkins wasn't enough, at least not in the long term. Finn was already looking for a way out. With her store. "Finn."

"Your father was going to sell his share to someone else, I outbid—"

"Me." She looked at his hand on her wrist and pulled back. She didn't scream. She didn't yell. Her body was completely shut down. "You outbid me. Liam set up a limited liability company for me. My brother put in the offer as soon as Dad started discussing it. I was purchasing Saddler's under that name." Three years of saving every paycheck, so that she could afford the down payment on the loan that would let her buy the company in the event her father wouldn't come around.

Years of planning. Her goal of showing everyone she could do it herself.

Gone. Just gone.

"Once we expand, are you planning on running the West Coast Division, while I manage the home office?" That was cruel, but the words were out before she could control herself.

"Dammit, Nat, how can you think I'd want to leave?" Finn ran his hands through his hair after he stepped towards her.

She stepped back. "Have appraisers been out to Nightfall?"

She knew the answer. This town was tiny. She'd heard about it last week. And tried to pretend that there was a good reason. A reason he hadn't told her.

"Yes, but, listen, Nat."

She didn't want excuses. "Do you still have a place in California?"

He'd traveled back every two weeks for three months. She hadn't asked if he'd put his house on the market. She kept hoping he might tell her he was relocating permanently. He said his place was here, but a large part of his life was still there.

And he's already planning to expand the store outside the state.

Those were the words she couldn't get passed. Owner for less than a day and already looking to grow so he could be somewhere else.

Finn bit his lip. "Yes, I still have my town home."

"So, you are hedging. Right? In case this doesn't work out? Or in case you get bored with Walkins?" She waited praying he'd argue. He promised to tell her before he went back to California, but he never truly promised to stay here. Never told her that this was enough.

It isn't. Not forever. How could it be?

She'd ignored the future. Ignored pinning him down on it. Left it alone to avoid this moment.

He'd always want more.

"Why didn't you tell me about your other company? Did you not trust me?" He took a deep breath. "I am not the only one keeping secrets here."

Finn's quiet words ripped through her final layer of

control as shame warred with anger. Her nerves were too raw to deal with this now. The day had been too long.

"Please leave," she articulated each syllable as she pointed to the open front door.

Her heart broke as Finn stepped across the threshold. He hadn't believed Natasha could buy Saddler's. He didn't think her grand plans were grand enough. He wanted more. Needed more.

She sank to the floor and let the sobs overtake her. It wasn't until the smoke detector activated that she finally stood to pull the crispy mess from her oven.

***

She didn't trust me enough to tell me Plan B. Didn't trust me to stay.

After everything, Nat believed Finn would want something else. Maybe not today or this year, but she didn't trust his plans to include her. How could he convince her his life was wherever she was? There was only one way to make sure she never doubted it. He grabbed his phone and made the first of several calls.

Mark picked him up at Nightfall forty-five minutes later. Slinging the small duffel bag into the back seat, Finn slid in.

"Thanks for agreeing to drive me to the airport. Warren's old truck needs more than a tune up, particularly after I sped most of the way here from the airport this morning. I'm afraid it would bust on the side of the highway if I took it again." Glancing at his watch, he tried to control the anxious energy bouncing through him. "It's going to be tight, but I should make the flight."

Mark kept his eyes on the road. "This is a bad idea, man. You're running after a fight."

Finn's stomach flipped, but he ignored the worry pressing

at the back of his brain. "I am not running. You know that. Did you set up the company for Natasha?"

Fear that Mark had kept Natasha's plans from him, even when he knew Finn planned to purchase Saddler's, worried him. Client privilege be damned, and if he'd known, he'd have never put in his offer.

Mark shook his head as he kept his eyes on the highway, "No, she and her brother must have gone with someone out of town. Less likely Herb catches wind of it that way." He let out a heavy sigh as he passed the eighteen-wheeler.

"Is something else bothering you?"

"Just wondering how Natasha is going to kill me when she finds out I took you to the airport." No trace of laughter coated Mark's comment.

Finn slapped his friend on the arm, "She's so mad at me, I doubt she will realize I'm gone. A day in and out. When we talk, I want to be able to prove that I'm not going anywhere."

"And selling everything in California is going to do that?"

"My company has already been sold. I'm just getting rid of a house I barely lived in, a car, and moving the bank accounts. Shouldn't take me anytime to get the house on the market. I had my assistant start looking for realtors and plan to meet one an hour after I land. The other two issues can be handled in under two hours. Then, red eye back." Not sure if he was trying to convince himself or Mark, Finn added, "I'll call Nat first as soon as I land to explain."

"And you expect Natasha to be angry enough to remain away from Nightfall, or to not call you?" Mark was making more than a few excellent points, but Finn's ticket was purchased, and this way he could demonstrate, tangibly, his desire to remain in Walkins.

He hoped she'd hear the excitement he had, when he mentioned expanding outside of the state. However, he could also see how she'd look at it as evidence that he wasn't fully committed to the future. If he was honest, this wasn't completely about Natasha. Finn was excited about the future for the first time in decades. Opening the tech training facility focused on agricultural needs gave him the same thrill he had in the early days of Reach. It was going to be successful.

Walkins had more to offer than his young eyes had been able to comprehend.

He wanted others to benefit from the lessons he'd learned in California without having to leave home, if they didn't want to travel so far. He had the capital to ensure complete ownership, and this venture would never be sold without his consent. *Complete ownership.*

That was what Nat wanted. The worry pressed against his brain. He could fix this.

"Walkins is home, but I understand why Natasha believes I want something else. I should have put the house on the market a month ago. I never planned to keep it. This frees up all my time to focus on my new adventure. The tech facility still needs a name. Maybe my lawyer can come up with one while I'm gone." Finn stepped from the car and tried to convince himself this was the right move.

"Send her a message and let her know she won't be able to reach you for a few hours. Otherwise, she might think you're gone for good. Don't give her a reason to think you're running," Mark called through the open window as Finn raced for the airport door.

"Thanks for the advice." Finn pulled up her number and stared at her profile picture. She'd been talking to someone else, smiling and starting to laugh when he'd snapped it.

It rang once and she sent it to voicemail. He listened to her voice tell him to leave a message, but the words stuck in his throat. He'd call her as soon as the wheels touched the ground. This fight was just a time out. A pause.

Everything would be easier when the last ties to his west coast life were severed.

Had he left any dough in the fridge? Nat pulled the door open and sighed as she grabbed the bowl. She dipped the large spoon into the chilled dough. One spoonful was all she was going to allow herself, maybe two. Lifting her phone, she stared again at the blank screen. What was she expecting to see? He'd called and she'd sent it to voicemail.

He hadn't left one. Sending him to voicemail was petty and Nat couldn't fault him for not leaving one. So, she'd typed out a quick message thirty minutes later telling him to give her a ring. She'd held the damn thing in her hand since she sent her simple text message.

It hadn't buzzed. Hadn't dinged. Hadn't done a damn thing. So, she knew Finn still hadn't responded. She hadn't answered his call, but surely, he wouldn't just ignore her. She might understand his anger, but she swallowed her pride and placed one more text.

'Please call me. I want to talk.'

Natasha chastised herself for typing out a text rather than giving Finn a call, but she hit send anyway. At the very least, she needed to tell him about the baby. Her eyes teared when she thought of raising their child without Finn.

That was tomorrow's problem. She had enough on her plate right now.

There was a knock at the door. She dropped the bowl and took off. She opened it and felt the world crash as Lauren stared back at her.

"You okay?" Lauren held up her hand as she headed to the sofa. "Dumb question."

"Yeah," Nat crossed her legs as she sat on the other end of the couch. "It's been a day. And the twenty-four hours isn't even over yet. Ridiculous. Finn and I fought. He's not answering his phone."

"Well, he can't have it on in the plane," Lauren rolled her neck and yawned.

"Airport?" The air in the room wasn't enough. The walls were closing. No. He'd sworn he'd tell her before he left.

I told him to leave.

Surely, he hadn't taken her seriously.

Lauren reached her hand across the sofa, resting it on her knee. "I am sorry Nat. I assumed when Mark cancelled our trip to the movies to take Finn to the airport that you knew about it."

"I never was enough to hold him here." Natasha cringed as the words slipped out. "Of course, I did my best to push him away this time."

Leave. She'd told him to leave. She couldn't blame him for taking her up on the offer. Gripping her phone, she checked, but he hadn't responded. *How can he? He's on a plane.*

Her soul cried as she typed out a final message and hit send. A box of tissues landed in her lap, and Natasha raised her head.

"I'm sorry." Her words hiccupped between sobs. "Guess I'm not great company?"

Lauren propped her feet up on the small coffee table and cocked her head at Natasha. "What happened?"

Swallowing the lump in her throat, Natasha relayed the day's events and then blew her nose. "Pathetic, I know."

"Not pathetic, prideful."

Natasha blinked. She'd expected comfort, but Lauren didn't look comforting. "What do you mean?"

"Finn should have told you about his bid for Saddler's."

"Of course, he needed to tell me, it's *my company.*" She heard herself and bit her lip. Once upon a time, she wanted to share it with him. He'd done that, and she'd gotten angry. Thrown him out.

Sighing, Lauren stood. "I am going to say something, and then, if you want me to leave, I will. Your father is right."

So everyone thought it. That stung.

"You can't do everything yourself, and you don't need to. Yes, Finn should have told you his plans, but you've been holding back from him, too. Fear and pride are going to ruin your second chance. You need to decide what you really want. I can't do that. and neither can Finn."

Natasha opened her mouth to argue and then closed it. "What happens if I want it all?"

"Life isn't about having it all, honey. It's about loving what you have." Lauren stood and headed for the door, but Natasha grabbed her hand.

"If I can get the last flight to California, can you take me to the airport?"

She'd told him to leave but that didn't mean she couldn't follow this time.

Chapter Sixteen

A BEEPING PHONE informed Finn that his battery life was exhausted, and he watched in horror as his cell phone powered itself off. He'd scoured the outside of the duplex, looking for any outlet. His spare key disappeared from the nook by her door.

Maybe she already changed the lock.

Giving up, he slid back against Natasha's door and prayed she didn't attempt to call him. Not that she'd reached out since her final text. For the first time in more than a decade, he was completely unreachable. When it really mattered, Nat had no way to get ahold of him if she tried.

Not that she'd answered any of my calls.

They'd all gone immediately to voicemail. Like she'd blocked his number. He was not giving into the bleakness. Not yet. 'Just come home, baby.'

The plea went unanswered in the empty corridor. The thoughts that had driven him back to Walkins less than five hours after he left came crashing back with no phone to provide distractions. Mark was right. His desire to give Natasha a day or so to calm down and, if he were honest, come to her senses, were wildly misplaced and selfish.

In his stupidity, he'd failed to alert the woman he loved to his intentions to return. He'd finally acted like his reckless parents, and it might have cost him everything. Nat texted her request to meet and talk while he was still on the plane. Apparently, word of his departure arrived before the plane touched down as her final message simply stated, "Goodbye. I wish you the best in California."

She'd failed to answer any of his calls. He had not even bothered to leave the airport. Booking the first flight that would get him back home and praying she'd pick up her phone were his only hopes. He rented the fastest car he could find. It hadn't mattered though.

She was gone.

Desperation gripped him. Perhaps Natasha was staying at Nightfall Ranch. Finn doubted it, but he needed to do something to find her. There were only so many places in Walkins where she might be. He grabbed his keys and stood.

The door to the corridor opened, "Nat? Nat?"

He leaned over the railing to see Lauren.

"So, you are here." Lauren paused as she moved to unlock Natasha's door.

"You're not Natasha."

"Perceptive. You're also lucky it's me watching Charcoal, and not Scarlett." Lauren slid past him and headed through Natasha's door.

"So, Scarlett was serious about shooting me. Not surprising." He might even welcome it if he couldn't figure out a way to fix this.

Lauren looked over her shoulder and shrugged. "I don't *think* Scarlett would shoot you, but I don't want to help hide a body."

"Fair enough." He was pretty sure Lauren meant that, too. "Where is Nat?"

After she placed the sack on the counter, the woman tipped her head to the side and motioned for him to sit.

"I've made a mess of this, Lauren. I need to talk to her."

That brought a smile to her lips, and she turned to open a can of food for the cat.

"Kitty." Charcoal came swiftly out of the bedroom, ignoring Finn's presence.

"Why are you feeding him? Where did Natasha go?"

She emptied the small tin into the cat dish and pulled two beers from her bag. Once more, she motioned for him to take a seat. "Have a drink with me, Finn."

"Are you going to tell me where Natasha is?"

Twisting the lid off her beer, Lauren took a deep sip. "Depends. You planning on leaving without telling her again?"

Finn shook his head, pursing his lips. "No. One time mistake."

"Big mistake." Lauren took another long sip.

"Please, tell me where she is. I will get in the car, or on a plane, a ship, whatever, to get to her. I need to fix this."

"I think enough people have gotten on a plane," Lauren smiled as she tapped the top of her drink to his.

Natasha raised her hands, wishing she'd remembered to throw her sunglasses in her purse. Heat rose against the asphalt, and she fanned herself ineffectively with a receipt she'd dug from the bottom of her purse. The smell of the masses and morning coffee threatened to overwhelm her, as she walked the blocks towards Finn's office.

What if he won't see me? Why won't he answer his phone? She'd started calling the moment she landed. Surely, he was here. Why wasn't his phone on? *Do I tell him about the baby? Why did I push him away?*

Cool air blasted her as she opened the door to Reach's downtown offices. Trendy furniture and glass decorations lined the professional lobby. Glancing at her rumpled look, it was easy to tell she was out of place.

"Excuse me." A young man balancing eight cups of coffee and a bag of bagels forced her to step closer to the front desk, which gained her the receptionist's attention.

The stunning brunette waited as Natasha tried to find the right words. "I need to see Finn."

The woman's smile faltered slightly at her rushed words. "There are several Finn's that work here. Can you be more specific?"

Heat flooded Natasha's face. The name tag plate positioned above the woman's desk read Ava, and Natasha took a deep breath, trying to focus.

"Ava," she said with what she hoped was a pleasant smile, "My name is Natasha Saddler. I need to see Mr. Matus. He founded this company."

Ava's eyes shifted to the right, and Natasha followed her gaze. Of course, the woman knew the company's founder. Several pictures of Finn hung on the wall. Of him cutting a ribbon on the building. Of him shaking important looking people's hands. Of him and Warren, taken when he'd won the senior science award. She'd been behind the camera that day. Finn brought a little part of her and Warren with him.

Ava offered a bright, false smile before gesturing for Natasha to take a seat in one of the silver chairs. The back bent as Natasha tried to relax. Were they designed to put guests on edge, or had no member of the staff sat in them?

"Mr. Matus's assistant will be with you shortly," Ava stated before turning her back to Natasha. His assistant, not Finn, was coming to collect her. Did that mean something? Was he planning to have an employee ask her to leave? Would she have to ask the assistant to tell Finn he was going to be a father?

Calm down. She was reading a million meanings into a

simple statement. Either Finn was willing to see her, or he wasn't. Either way, tomorrow would come.

Her phone buzzed with a rushed reply. 'Nat. My phone died. Bad excuse, I know. My assistant is coming to get you. Just stay in the lobby."

The text landed, and she let out a cry. Before she could respond an efficient looking young woman stepped up. "Ms. Saddler, I am Katiya Belov, Mr. Matus' assistant."

She extended her hand and Natasha reached for it. "Please call me Natasha. Finn just texted me. He said you were coming to get me."

Katiya smiled, "Follow me. We have Mr. Matus online in his office."

The elevator doors slid shut, and Natasha intentionally didn't ask what Katiya's statement meant. The elevator doors opened, and Katiya gave Natasha a small smile. The plush carpet silenced their walk towards Finn's office. Several doors were open and boxes were stacked in all.

"Is the whole office moving?"

Katiya kept walking but looked over her shoulder and smiled. "With the sale of the company, most of the original board is moving on or retiring."

"You don't sound worried?" Surely, Finn had informed her he wasn't staying with Reach post-sale. Katiya seemed happy though. Perhaps Finn's assistant already had plans?

She opened the door at the end of the office and motioned for Natasha to follow her. "I'm looking forward to my next adventure. He's expecting you."

After sliding Natasha inside, Katiya left. A few boxes were stacked next to the door, but it was the chair facing the empty back wall that held Natasha's attention. "I'm sorry, Finn. I overreacted. That's an understatement, I know but, I'm still scared I won't be enough. Competing with this?"

She gestured to the office surrounding her, which was far grander than the little building she'd walked into years ago.

"Honey, of course you're enough. I'm sorry I ever made you feel that wasn't the case."

She jumped as Finn's voice came from the wall behind her. His face was plastered across a large flat screen.

"What the?" Natasha walked to the desk and spun the empty chair. "Where are you?"

His eyes crinkled on the wall as she walked towards him. He looked tired and worried. "Somewhere I wish I could touch you. I came home."

"What?" She traced his chin with her finger. "I went to your home before I came here. Why didn't you answer the door?"

He moved back away from the camera, and she stared at Nightfall's kitchen.

Home, he'd used the word to describe Walkins. Her heart burst with love as she stared at the faded paint in their kitchen. *Our kitchen.*

"You came back?" Tears leaked down her cheeks as she lovingly caressed the flat screen.

"I will always come back. I want to believe that I bought Saddler's to help you, but truthfully, I wanted a reason that you had to keep me."

"Finn," Nat's fingers brushed over his chin. "I'm so sorry. You can be my partner in anything. I was so focused on doing it myself. I let the joy of having you as my partner blind me. I love you."

"I love you, too. Come home," Finn's hand covered the screen. He was tracing her image, just like she was.

She placed a kiss against the glass. Stepping back, she looked at him and held her hands over her belly. That was a conversation that should wait. "Can I use a computer here to book a flight?"

"You are on the one o'clock." Jumping, Natasha raised a hand to her warm cheek. She kept her back to Finn as he laughed.

"She does that to me all the time." Finn's chuckle filled the room and she joined in.

Reaching for the piece of paper in Katiya's hand, Natasha calculated she had approximately five hours before she was standing in Finn's arms based on the travel itinerary the woman handed her. "Thank you. Side note, those chairs in your lobby are terrible."

Finn winked, "I know, but they aren't my problem anymore. Reach is fully owned and operated by Smith, Anderson, and Joveston International. We own Saddler's and a tiny tech education facility in Wyoming."

Natasha stared at him. "What?"

"I promise to give you all the details, in person, after I have made love to you." Finn winked again, and Natasha glared at him before turning to apologize to Katiya.

"Where'd she go?"

"Told you she was a master. Go get in the car that Katiya no doubt has waiting. My phone is fully charged, and we can talk the whole way to the airport. Love you."

"Love you, too," she called as she trotted out of the room.

<h1 style="text-align:center">Chapter Seventeen</h1>

Finn kept his eyes focused on the arrivals list in Cheyenne's main hub. He'd been at the airport for over an hour. Nothing was stopping him from seeing her the second she walked past the secured area. The plane had arrived fifteen minutes ago. This airport wasn't that big. More than one person headed to the carousel to pick up their belongings. So, where was Nat?

Finn strained his neck as another group of people walked out.

Another group without her.

He grabbed his phone. She texted that they were on the ground but nothing since. All he wanted was her in his arms. The last twenty-four hours was the most surreal of his life, and he wanted no more of it.

Finally, Nat rounded the corner, an older woman walking next to her. The two were chatting and getting on like old friends. Nat met his gaze across the distance and waved while her companion continued to chitter away.

As they walked up, the woman patted her hand. "Remember, ginger will do amazing things for that morning sickness."

Nat looked at him, her mouth open as the elderly woman's family walked up and she left.

"Morning sickness?" Their first time together. Finn added the weeks up.

Nat was pregnant.

"I had planned a different way to tell you. I actually didn't tell her the reason I raced to the bathroom as soon as the flight ended." Nat looked at the bouquet in his hands. "Sunflowers. My favorite."

He dropped to his knee. He'd also planned something different, but he didn't want to wait another minute.

"Finn?"

"Marry me, Nat." He pulled the ring from his back pocket.

"Is that?" She bit her lip and pushed a tear away, "Is that my ring?"

"Mostly. New diamond in the center, but the old one was cut to make the side stones. Past and future. Say yes, honey. Please."

"Oh, yes." She laughed, "Of course it's yes."

He slid the ring on her finger and picked her up. "I love you so much."

"I love you, too." She pressed her lips to his.

There was clapping in the background from strangers who'd witnessed the moment.

"No long engagement this time, okay?" She giggled as he set her down. She lay a hand over her flat belly. "Mostly joking."

He cupped her cheek. The fact that he hadn't set a date last time was not a mistake he planned to make again. "You want a big ceremony?"

If that was what she wanted, he'd move heaven and earth to make it happen—quickly. Her nose scrunched. "Not really. I want my family there."

"Your definition of family includes most of Walkins." He didn't begrudge her that, but it meant a couple hundred people at a minimum.

"So?" She stuck her tongue out. "Lauren is an ordained

minister. Something she got online for Scarlett's ceremony. She can marry us in the park, and whoever can make it, can make it."

"Is that what you want?"

"Yes, why?"

"Great. Two weeks? Or three from now?"

She let out a laugh. "Seriously? Like seriously?"

"I'd do it this weekend, but that might be asking a lot of people." He winked.

Nat slid into him, wrapping her arms around his neck. "Not if we send out a mass text, after I ask Scarlett to be my maid of honor. I assume you'll ask Mark to stand by you. And we need to tell my dad and brothers. Then the text can go to everyone else."

"Your wish is my command." He bent his head, capturing her lips. Nat. Home.

He'd chased his dreams and still found his way back.

To her.

To them.

To their child.

To us.

To their second chance at forever.

Epilogue

THE RAPID FIRE of a needle piercing his skin sounded against the quiet room. His skin was sore, but he had no plans to admit he was uncomfortable. Risking a quick glance at his watch, Finn realized he'd been in the chair for less than an hour.

"I saw that." Natasha rubbed her enlarged belly and laughed. "I warned you that piece was too big for a first tattoo."

Waddling over, she leaned over his shoulder to stare at the art taking form on his back. Their child kicked, and Finn placed a kiss against her belly. "I'm fine, and the piece is not that big." Finn ignored the artist's scoff. "You're just jealous that it's me in the chair and not you."

Grinning, she leaned back to rub the small of her back. "I swear, your child is determined to make everything ache these days."

When their child was kicking or behaving, Natasha lovingly cooed what a good boy or girl they were being. The second she had to pee after midnight, her feet swelled, or her back ached was when the child became his. Finn wouldn't have it any other way.

They'd decided to wait to find out the baby's sex, but privately, Finn suspected it was his daughter making her mother's back ache. Their due date was only a week away, and he knew Nat was uncomfortable. "We can leave, if you want."

"The outline isn't done yet." Gareth, Nat's tattoo artist, did not hide his annoyance.

"He doesn't understand what that means," Nat giggled.

Finn barely resisted the urge to shrug. Gareth likely would grumble if Finn's movements messed up such artistry. Finn had asked for a design to represent coming home. He had stared at the tree of life, its root spelling, *Life takes you unexpected places, love brings you home,* for an hour the first time he saw it. As much as he longed for the permanent reminder, he hadn't counted on the pain. "How do you have so many of these?"

"Women tolerate pain better," Gareth muttered as he drew the machine across Finn's back. Finn kept his eyes on Natasha. Her cheeks were pink-stained, and her hands hadn't left her back for several minutes.

"Honey?"

"Sorry, baby brain. My mind feels foggy these days." She shifted a little, but her hands never left her back. "I can't get comfortable. I'm going to go walk a little. I figure you're in that seat for at least another three hours."

She winked, but Finn saw the flash of pain cross her face as she walked out of the small room. "How long until the outline is done, Gareth?"

"I only need about another twenty minutes for the outline. We can add in the details later. You think your kid's birthday is today?"

"She is trying to hide it, but yeah, I think so." Finn focused on the soft taps of Natasha's pacing and found the sting in his shoulder drift away. Twenty minutes later, she stopped as if on cue to lean against the wall.

"Finn!"

Luckily Gareth had finished the last line as Finn jumped from his seat at her call. Gareth followed, spraying Finn's shoulder and rubbing a paper towel across it.

"My water broke, or I just had a very unfortunate accident," Natasha's eyes were wide as she looked from Finn to Gareth. "I think we have to go. Outline done?"

"He finished the outline just before you yelled. I even grabbed my shirt."

Gareth pressed a film to Finn's back. "He's ready. You tell him how to care for this. And good luck."

Time moved swiftly, and drug along, as Natasha focused on bringing their child into the world. Hours later, as Finn's wife slept, and he held his tiny, sleeping daughter, he wondered how Gareth might feel about adding his daughter's initials to the roots of the tree.

www.ingramcontent.com/pod-product-compliance
Lightning Source LLC
Chambersburg PA
CBHW070752160726
48004CB00001B/158